By Barbie Scott

Chapter 1

I sat in my bathroom, on my gold toilet seat with my head in my hands. I was stressed the fuck out. I looked up and admired the framed picture of Scarface that was hanging in my bathroom. He was smoking a cigar while laying in the tub. I was beyond furious. The more I thought about it, the more it pissed me off. Therefore, I got out of the tub and headed into my bedroom. I went straight to my closet, grabbing my 9-millimeter with the silencer, and tucked it behind my back. I slid into my black Ugg boots and headed straight to the kitchen. I dumped all the bricks into a duffle bag I had just copped, and even threw the work inside the bag I was in the process of cooking, Pyrex jar and all. I hopped in my G-Wagon and made my way onto I 95 and headed to this nigga Esco's mansion.

Esco had sold me some work that was turning yellow and yellower, the more it cooked. At first, I thought I was tripping so I had cooked up a brick, and then another one. The more I cooked it, the more it lost. Every ounce I dropped on my triple beam scale let me know I was assed out on twenty-six thousand dollars and this nigga was going to have to answer to this shit.

Esco wasn't no small-time nigga, as a matter of fact, he was that nigga, so I knew I had to carry my words wisely or I'd be leaving out that bitch in a body bag. The only upper hand he had on me was that I was going to be in his place of residence and his security was on point. I didn't give a fuck, business was business, and when it came to my money anybody could get it.

When I pulled up to the security booth, the blonde head security called up to Esco and told him I was there. Clear as day, I could hear Esco through the monitor, telling him to let me thru the gates.

When I pulled in, there were all kinds of whips parked out front, from Bentley's to Ferrari's. This nigga crib was something like I had seen in the movies I watched when I was younger. Twenty-six bedrooms, an Olympic sized pool, and 3 kitchens. This Mexican motherfucker was living large. Now, don't get it twisted, I was doing great for myself at 26 years old. I had a six-bedroom home, three dens, seven bathrooms, a pool, jacuzzi, basketball court, and four whips I could drive for whatever mood I was in. Before I forget to mention, NO MAN and NO KIDS, and didn't plan on having either of the two anytime soon.

My name is Cash Lopez, and yes, Cash is the name that was written in bold letters across my birth records. My mom was a full blown hustler, and I guess she had it bad for cash. At 5'7, 165 pounds, which is mostly in my ass, and some size C cup tits, I didn't need any babies fucking up my body or any man stressing me out. They were going to have me looking like them skinny, crack head nigga diet ass bitches, so it was just me and my puppy, Gutta. My caramel complexion and long hair came from my mother who was one hundred percent Puerto Rican. People said I favored the model Bernice Burgos, I WAS THAT BITCH!

"What the fuck is this, Esco?" I said. I slammed my duffle bag on the table in front of him.

He looked up at me and stood to his feet. "Cash, I do apologize, there was a mix up with the work. I'm going to give you back all your money and I'll have more product for you in two days," he said with his heavy accent.

My face softened a little. I was glad he owned up to his mistake. He was a solid dude, so I was sure he was going to run me back every dime of the $312,000 dollars I had spent.

He handed me a duffle bag full of cash, which was confirmation that he knew I was coming back.

Esco and I had been doing business for years. Ever since my mother got popped by the Feds and was up north doing 15 years. I grabbed the bag and told him to call me as soon as he copped, I and made my way towards the door.

On my way out, I bumped into a sexy ass nigga who eye fucked me the minute we ran into each other. However, he quickly stepped around me and headed straight to Esco. From where I stood, I could hear him going off about the work. He was a sexy ass nigga, I couldn't front. He was so sexy, he actually made my coochie jump at just the sight of him.

He was about 6'2 with dreadlocks that hung to the middle of his back. He was thick as hell and looked so much like this sexy ass nigga name EJ Adams from ATL that I'd saw on Instagram. He was rocking a white V-neck that hugged his biceps and some True Religion jeans that hung low, showing off his Polo boxer briefs. His chain swung side to side as he walked, and I could tell he was heated by the frown on his face.

He was so fine, I was stuck at the entrance of the door, watching him. When we locked eyes, he smiled at me and boy, I was so embarrassed.

I headed out to my truck. I reached behind my back for my strap. I turned on my air conditioner and put my foot on the brakes twice, then my stash popped out. I made sure Dolly was secure in her stash before I headed back home to get some rest.

When I pulled up to my crib, I noticed a dark blue Benz sitting in front of my home because for sure, it couldn't get past security. I pulled up to my gate and pulled out my iPhone 6. I entered my gate's security code so I could pull in. I saw a figure appear from the car and heading in my direction. I grabbed Dolly out the stash and waited for whoever it was to get closer. If I didn't know who it was, I was going to put some hot led in their ass.

"What the fuck you doing at my house, Ricky?" I asked, getting out my car the minute I realized who it was.

"Why the fuck is you not answering my calls, Cash?"

"Nigga, it doesn't matter, why the fuck you popping up at my fucking house? You know damn well I don't play that shit."

He roughly grabbed my arm, I could tell he was pissed. "What the fuck you hiding, ma?"

"Boy, I'm not hiding shit. You not my nigga so don't pop up to my fucking house, nigga."

I was mad as a muthafucka. This nigga knew better. This was exactly why I was single because I didn't want to answer to anybody.

Ricky was an around the way D-Boy that peddled a little dope. Nothing major, but he was sexy as fuck and had dick for eternity. I didn't give a fuck, it took more than just good dick for a bitch in my caliber. I'm sorry, but he just wasn't that nigga. I had plenty dudes and didn't plan on settling down anytime soon.

"Ms. Lopez, are you ok?" Pedro asked me, appearing out of the dark.

Pedro was my top security and had been working with me for some time. He was my mom's right-hand man when she was heavy in the streets. However, when she got knocked, he vowed to her he would always look after me. Pedro was a hitman for some top Cartel's, but retired after his wife and seven-year-old son was murdered, so I put him on my payroll. Out of the four guards I had, he was the one I trusted the most with my life.

"Yes, Pedro, I'm fine, thank you."

He gave me an uneasy look and stepped back by the gate, but didn't move until I moved.

"So you gonna act like that with a nigga, Cash?" Ricky asked, but I gave him a look that said get the fuck from in front of my house and he did just that.

He stomped his way to the car just like the little bitch he was. I didn't give a fuck about his feelings, pop-ups were a no-no, straight the fuck up.

I jumped in my whip and pulled in my gate. Pedro stood there until the gate was secure.

When I got in the house, I headed to my room for a shower. I had a long day ahead of me and today was already a long one. Tomorrow, I was meeting with my girls at *Juice* for a great time of popping bottles and watching my money make more money.

Juice was a club I owned that I put my heart into. I put every dollar I had into my club when I first came into the game.

Now see, I wasn't no dumb bitch, I washed my money the minute I made too much to count by hand. I had my club and an all-female barbershop called *Trap Gyrl* that had the city lit. On Friday nights, I ran the strip club with female strippers, male exotic dancers on Saturday's, and every regular night, it was a regular crowd but with lingerie waitress.

Don't call me crazy, call me a hustler. I knew the right shit to invest in that would be different than all other businesses. I knew what was popular, and I knew what made money.

My establishments were unique. I also had the baddest bitches hustling for me, not working for me, but hustling for me because no matter how you got it, it was all a hustle.

I eased down into the hot water in my jacuzzi tub, relaxed my head on the headrest, and closed my eyes. I slowly dozed off and was awoken by the sound of my Drake "Right Hand" ringtone. I knew it was my girl, so I dried my hands on the nearest towel and answered.

"Hello?"

"What's the deal, biaaatch?"

"Hey, ma," I said smiling at my girl, Malina.

Malina had the bubbliest personality, but she was a gangsta at heart. She wasn't into the streets up until she met me, and I made her into a true hustler. Don't get me wrong, she was a hustler and gangsta before I met her, she just never affiliated in the street life much. Her brother was a stick-up kid that was now upstate serving a bid and he was my goon from back in the days.

The first time me and Malina met, we hit it off immediately. It was something about her I took a liking to, therefore, I put her under my wing, making her my right hand.

"I was just seeing what's up, I'm not doing shit. I went by the trap three and four to collect. I'm finally home, about to take a bath, and call a skeez."

I couldn't help but laugh because she was just like me in so many ways. As much as we always said *fuck niggas,* we still hated sleeping alone.

"Ugh, bitch, I don't even wanna talk about that. Ricky punk ass popped up at my fucking house."

"Oh my God, you're lying?"

"I wish I was. Ugh, that shit turned me off."

"I know it did. Ah, hell naw, pop-ups are a no-no, yo," Malina said, sounding serious as hell.

I couldn't have agreed more.

"So, what you do?"

"Girl, damn near drew down on his ass," I said while laughing. "Nah, I told his punk ass to slide, and I wasn't feeling that shit. He stormed off like a fucking brat."

"Oh, no, that nigga is crazy. So, we on tomorrow or nah?"

"Hell yeah, I gotta holla at Que and get the math for trap 1 and 2, and then hit the mall."

"Ooh, your boo?" Malina giggled.

"Girl, you know I ain't checking for Que ass like that. He could keep giving me that good swipe and keep it pushing," I said.

We both start laughing.

Que was my right hand man, next to Malina, that ran two of my traps. He really did his own thing. He was my mother's lieutenant and it was her empire, he was left to work for me. He was a sexy chocolate nigga that wore his hair cut low with waves. He also had dimples to die for. His body was right and covered in tattoos. He was a hoe ass nigga, though.

He was like all hoe ass niggas. But, the minute I ever say let's be together, he would drop them bitches left and right, I just wasn't ready. I for sure wasn't ready to wife a nigga that I would have to body because his hoe ass had bitches flocking like bluebirds and I wasn't having that shit.

"Aight, well, call me when you get up. I need to do some shopping too," Malina said, sounding tired.

"Ok, I'll hit you at about nine."

"Ok, ma, good night."

"Good night." I pressed end and dropped my phone on the side of the tub.

After relaxing for about thirty minutes, I lathered up with my Pretty in Pink and got out. I went to my bed and laid down naked. I grabbed my book Straight from the Gutta by Robin Chanel and read until I dozed off.

***

When I opened my eyes, it was 7:30 in the morning. I had to meet Que, so I took a quick shower and then went downstairs to feed Gutta. I slipped into a Pink sweatsuit, my pink Nike Cortez, and brushed my hair back into a slick ponytail, letting it hang long. I kept it simple with my diamond studs and Rolex watch. I overlooked myself in my full-length mirror and headed out the door.

On my way to the car, I noticed Pedro by the tennis court working out. I motioned to him with my hand that I'll be back.

He nodded and waved back, saying ok.

I jumped in my chrome Benz and threw on my Blueprint 1 CD, and then hopped on the highway.

My Nicki Minaj Your Love ringtone chipped. Rolling my eyes, but smirking, I answered on the second ring.

"Sup, Que?"

"Sup, wife?" Que said, calling me by his little nickname he gave me.

"On my way to you now."

"Alright, I was just making sure you was up."

"Yeah, I went to sleep kinda early."

"Whaaat? You must didn't have one of them bum ass niggas in yo bed last night."

"Oh my God, Que, don't start. I'm pulling up, bye," I said while hanging up. It was too early for that shit and it was bad enough I wasn't a morning person.

When I pulled up, there was a BMW sitting out front. I pulled down the street and walked towards the trap. Que was leaned on the car and the minute I walked up, the girl mugged me but I didn't pay that hoe no mind. That bitch wouldn't even make it off the block if she even thought about getting buck. That's the one thing I hated about Que's little groupies, them bitches didn't know their place. Que would slap the shit out of a bitch for me and that's what they hated the most. Bitches stayed questioning him about us fucking and no lie, we were but even if we weren't, they would still get put on all fours. Truth was, Que would body any bitch or nigga for me, but these silly bitches not knowing what kind of operation we were running, they thought otherwise.

It was a couple of his females that were cool and got a chance to chill with the team. They were the hoes that knew their place in his life, the silly bitches got fucked and shook, and that's exactly what it was.

I walked past the car, headed into the house, and straight to the back where I knew I could find Blaze. Blaze was Que's lieutenant. He was quiet as a motherfucker, handled his business, and would kill on instinct. Blaze was somebody I could trust with my life. As they say, you got to watch them quiet motherfuckers.

Any situation that went bad, they never expected Blaze to turn up, but he was the one that kept the chopper and would split a nigga wig while holding a poker face.

I got straight to work since Que was outside playing Mack Daddy of the year.

"What's up, Cash?" Blaze said as he looked up from the money counter. He had a blunt hanging from his lips and kept a steady face.

"Shit, what's the deal, Blaze, you got that ready for me?"

"Yep, just about. Them three bags are done," he pointed to the floor where three duffle bags sat.

"Ok, well, I'm going to make the deposit since Que outside macking and not working."

He laughed. "Damn, you sound mad?"

"Boy, ain't nobody sweating Que's hoe ass."

He gave me that *yeah, ok* look, and continued his counting.

Que walked in smirking like he heard our conversation, but I didn't pay his ass any mind.

"Sup, Wifey?"

"Nothing, nigga. I'm going to make the drop and head to the mall."

"Word? Can I roll?"

"No, nigga, yo crazy ass ain't going with me!"

We all laughed.

14

"Aight, well, buy me something. I'm coming tonight and you know I gotta get dougie."

"I'll think about it," I said. I got up and grabbed two bags. "Grab them other two bags, Que, and bring them out for me."

He grabbed the bags and came out behind me, talking shit the whole way, as usual. We put the bags in my trunk and before I could get in, he hemmed me up against the car.

"When you gon' stop playing, Cash, and let me take care of you?"

"When you get your dick checked and eighty-six all ninety-nine bitches you have," I said sarcastically and got in my car.

He just laughed and shook his head.

I turned my ignition, revved my engine, and smiled at him while I pulled off.

When me and Malina made it to the mall, we went straight for Vicky Secret and then Saks. We flirted with a few guys. I even gave my number to some cute as nigga with braids and tattoos. Baby was fine and looked like he was getting dough. Now, I wasn't a gold digger, but the cash I was getting, I needed a nigga on my level. I didn't tell men what I did for a living or what I owned, I just let them think whatever or I would simply say I was a real estate agent.

We went to the food court to eat, and I noticed two chicks that we had seen in Saks, mad dogging. They took a seat at the booth behind us and stared us down until Malina got right in on them bitches.

"Umm, do you bitches have a problem?" Malina asked.

They started laughing like something was funny.

"As a matter fact, I do," one of the bitches with a long ass weave said, looking at me.

"Well, bitch, address your issue because a bitch like me don't have time for thot ass hoes."

"Thot?" her friend said, getting mad.

That's when the long weave girl spoke again.

"I'm just going to get to the point. Are you fucking Que?"

Que? I said to myself while laughing.

Now, normally I wouldn't do no shit like this, but this hoe was beside herself.

"Bitch, why you worried about it? Ask Que! Better yet, let me call him so you can ask him," I said pulling out my phone.

Before I knew it, the bitch was getting up and heading towards me. But before she could reach me, I leaped up and two pieced the hoe.

"Bitch, I'm gon show you why not to fuck with me!" I was yelling repeatedly while punching the bitch over and over.

Malina jumped in and we stomped the hoe out. Her friend didn't do shit but stand there holding her mouth open. Security broke us up. I was beyond furious.

"I'm going to catch you again, bitch, so you betta watch your back," she said while security was holding us back.

"Bitch, the only place you gon catch me is in Que bed, and I'll be there tonight, hoe!"

"Yeah, tell that nigga I'm pregnant while you over there, bitch! I'm going to catch you, hoe. Watch, I'ma catch you!"

"Bitch, you can meet me outside right now," I said while trying to break free from security.

I was mad as a muthafucka. I couldn't believe this bum bitch had me out of character, and on tops, Que wasn't even my nigga and here it was, I was out here getting dirty over his ass. This was exactly one of the reasons I couldn't fuck with him like that. Now I regret ever even giving him my pussy. I couldn't wait to call his punk ass and give him a piece of my mind.

Malina and I walked to the car and got in. I circled the mall parking lot three times before we pulled out because security was on us heavy. I was trying find these hoes, I wasn't done.

I checked myself in the mirror, I had a scratch under my chin. Nothing serious, but I hated my face being scratched up.

"Man, I'ma fuck Que up, watch," Malina said as she looked in the mirror.

"Girl, you too? He a hoe ass nigga, Nina," I said, calling Malina by her nickname I gave her.

"Man, she's lucky I wasn't by my nine, yo. I probably would've shot the hoe," Nina said.

We both laughed.

"Let's go to Trap Gyrl and get touched up," I said, referring to our hair because it was all over the place.

My phone started ringing, it was Que. However, but I was so mad, I sent his ass to voicemail. I was going to press his ass when I saw him. So, for now, I was about to enjoy my day and get ready for *Juice* tonight. It was a regular club night so I had to be in full effect and enjoy myself at the same time.

When we got to the shop, I noticed all the ladies working while Lil Wayne's song "She Will" bumped thru the speakers. Then, I noticed Nikki, my hairdresser, wasn't in her booth so I went to my office to look over my books and calculated my earnings for the week.

"Hey, Cash," my barber, Monique said while waving.

Monique was a cute redbone with a nice shape and cute smile. She had been hustling for me for about three years and she had major clientele. She came to me after a fight with her ex-boyfriend Devon and told me that had enough of his abusiveness. She had run away from him when I bumped into her at club Juice and she asked me for a job. She had her cosmetology license and she was cute, so I gave her a chance, knowing she'd rack up on tips. Mo was an around the way thot and fucked fifty percent of her clients but she did what she had to do and got her money, so I let her do her.

"Hey, Mo?" I smiled. "You coming to work tonight or are you beat?"

"Girl, you know I'm coming. I'm going leave at six to go shower and I'll be there about nine tonight, you know, it's all money in," she laughed.

"I already know, boo. Where's Nikki?"

"She went to pick up our lunch."

"Ok… well, tell her I'll be in my office, I need a touch-up."

When I looked up, Nina was at the pool table shooting pool with some ugly, thick ass nigga. He looked like Mr. T in all that damn gold. I shook my head, giggled, and headed into my office.

After about an hour of counting, Nikki finally dragged her ass back in. She was rushing me like she had a million clients.

Nikki was the only hairdresser in the shop that had her own booth that ducked off in the back of the shop with her own Plasma TV. I had a surround sound so you could hear music throughout the entire shop so she was good on music.

Nikki was bad too. She was light skin, slim with a short cute cut that made her slim cheek bones stand out. She had a pretty set of teeth and she too was hustling at the club after she left the shop.

I sat in the chair, and she put the apron around me, getting ready to go to work. I looked down and admired my aprons, they were cute as hell with a skirt bottom. The logo was a sexy silhouette of a lady holding a money bag. The walls in the shop were red and trimmed in gold. The entire shop was painted with red walls, red and white flooring, and gold trimming. I had six plasmas, a wine machine, two X-box's, two PlayStation, and mirrors throughout the entire place. I had the Trap Gyrl logo in the middle of the floor and I let all my barbers sign their names around it. All the girls that didn't work for me anymore, I crossed their names out and I reminded all my girl that if they bit my hand, their names would to be crossed out quick, fast, and in a hurry.

"You coming out tonight, Ms. Thang?" Nikki said, snapping me out my day dream.

"Yeah, I'm coming. Are you working?"

"Hell yeah, I gotta finish paying for Niy's college tuition."

Niy was Nikki's oldest daughter and on her way to college to be a Law student. She was eighteen years old and doing great. I was so proud of her, I was also proud of Nikki.

Nikki had a perfect family. She had three kids and a great husband, except the fact he hated both her jobs. I never understood why she was working so hard because Marvin was a stockbroker and was rolling in cash. But for her, I guess she wanted her own money, and I wasn't mad at her.

"Aww, I'm miss my baby," I said in a whining tone.

"Me too, girl, I can't believe she leaving," Nikki said, then got she quiet.

"Girl, you bet not be stressing."

"Nah, I'm good, ma," she laughed.

"She'll be back, boo."

"Oh my God. Here this in love ass bitch go," Nikki said out of the blue.

I was curious because there wasn't anybody right there but me and her. I knew for sure she wasn't talking about Mwah.

"Who you talking about, hoe?"

"Girl, Mo, ol in love ass, playing this damn Nicki and Meek Mill song a million times."

We both started laughing.

"Who this bitch in love with now?"

"Girl, some fine ass D-boy she met a couple weeks ago. Got her ass open like 7-11!"

We both fell out laughing and continued with my hair.

Que was blowing my phone up nonstop, so I was sure his little bitch had told him what happened. I still ignored his ass and finished chopping it up with Nik until we were done.

I waited for Nina to get whipped up, and then we headed out to my house. Nina had her bags with her so she was getting dressed at my house. Therefore, we were about to get lit before we left.

Chapter 2

Twelve o'clock sharp when we arrived at Juice and it was already lit. The place was packed and the crowd was chill but turnt up. Hot Nigga was bumping thru the speakers as we made our way upstairs to the VIP so we can turn up our damn selves.

Me and Nina was shutting it down like always. I rocked a white halter dress with my cocaine white fur coat and my white Steve Madden heels. Nikki had hooked my hair back up with a part down the middle and feathered curls that I ran my fingers through, pushing it off my face. Nina had on her signature all black, some black Robin Jeans, and a black crop top. Her black fur coat complemented her black Louboutin's. Her hair was straight with a side part and light brown highlights.

We sat down and waited for the other girls to arrive. We poured our cups and talked until they came. Diane walked in with her sexy strut, looking like a million bucks. Whatever she was wearing, I knew it had to cost a fortune because anything she rocked costed an arm and leg.

Diane was getting money in a major way. She was a lawyer with her own firm, so on top of her making her own money, I kept her pockets fat. She had all the inside plugs to the DA's, Judges, and the dirty ass cops that we had to watch out for. Pedro had hired a few cops to hold us down, so we were straight when it came to the pigs.

"Come on, bitches, let's go dance," Diane said while dancing in her spot.

We laughed because the bitch wasn't here three minutes and was already ready to turn up. We grabbed a bottle off the table and headed downstairs to the dance floor.

On my way out, I told Big Mike, the bouncer, to let the girls know we were here and going to shake our asses.

When we reached the bottom, it was packed. We mingled our way thru the crowd and danced all the way thru until we found a spot to post up.

"Shout out to the Trap Gyrlz, in the building," DJ Bounce announced over the mic.

He played my theme song, Beyonce's "Diva," and me and my girls went up. I popped the bottle of champagne I was holding and took a swig, making sure I didn't get a drop on my white.

"Divas!" Tiny and Niya was shouting, coming towards us.

It was really time to show our asses. I took off my coat and hung it over my shoulder, but not missing a beat.

We partied, flirted, and eye fucked a few niggas until…
"Cash!"

I heard my name being called. It was Que storming my way like he was mad.

"I know you saw me fucking calling you, you always on some bullshit! Any fucking thing could've been wrong, Cash," he said, sounding mad and shaking his head.

"First off, get your fucking hands off me," I said snatching away from him. "Second, I'm not your bitch so stop yelling at me. Third, what you gotta say so important, Que? I'm listening."

He shook his head again before speaking. "Look, ma, I'm sorry about what happened today. That bitch ain't shit, and I checked her ass about that shit."

"Checked her? Nigga, I'm going to bust that bitch shit open when I see her, so tell her that! Oh, and by the way, I hope I didn't kill yall baby," I laughed.

"Man, that ain't my fucking baby."

"Que, I'm not your bitch, you ain't gotta lie or explain shit to me."

"I'm not explaining shit to you, I'm just telling you. And, why the fuck you all on the dance floor like you not a million-dollar bitch? Don't you know one of these niggas will love to snatch your ass up? You wilding, ma," he shook his head.

"You see that?" I pointed at all six guards that had their eyes on me, and tapped the inside of jacket pocket, letting him know I had Dolly on me.

He shook his head and walked off.

25

Therefore, me and my bitches continued to party until we were tired. We then heading back upstairs.

When we reached the top, a four pack of niggas was coming out the section across from us and immediately got in on me and my girls.

"You sexy as a muthafucka," one of the guys said. He grabbed my hand and spun me around.

"Thank youuu," I cooed.

"You're welcome. Here, put yo number in my phone," he said while reaching into his pocket.

"Nah, playa, she ain't putting shit in your phone," Blaze said as he walked up to us.

I could see Que in his seat, looking our way. He was smirking like he found the scene amusing.

"Blaze, damn, stop cramping my style," I mean mugged him, but he didn't budge.

Ol' boy looked like he was about to buck, but he thought against it when he noticed it was a crew of niggas surrounding him.

"My bad, homie, this you?"

"Don't worry about all that, just keep it moving."

He looked like he was about to say some slick shit, but followed his better judgment and did just that.

When I walked in my VIP section, Que was sitting down. There was some caramel chick all in his face and that shit had me hot. I wasn't jealous or anything, I was mad because these niggas cock blocked me every chance they got, but it was cool for them to stick their dicks in everything with a coochie and deep throat.

I sat at the table with my girls and they laughed because the whole time, I was grilling Que's ass, sending him death eyes. I could tell he felt uneasy because every girl that walked up on him, he told them to shoot like they were flies. I sat back, sipped my drink, and laughed at Niya's ass. She was all in Blaze's personal space and he was grilling her like he wanted her out his face.

"Girl, he act like he on dick," Niya said, coming over and taking a seat.

Niya wanted Blaze bad, but he didn't budge and it only made her want him more. No matter how hard she tried, he was not fucking with her. Blaze was the mean type. He didn't give a fuck about how sexy you were or how fat your ass was, he was all about his business. Nothing Niya could do or say would make him want her.

Niya was bad, hands down. Her chocolate complexion, fat ass, and flat stomach turned heads on a daily, but it was something about her Blaze just wasn't fucking with.

"Girl, you know Blaze ain't fucking with your ass."

"He be acting like I don't exist, Cash, and that shit drives me crazy."

"Why are you on him so tough?"

"I don't know, really. He's fine as fuck, I think it's his gangsta ass attitude that attracts me to him. I'm going to get his ass one day, watch. And if his dick wack, I'm going to tell everybody!" Niya said, and we both started laughing.

"Just give Que some pussy so he can leave me alone," I said, and I meant every word.

"Ugh, hell no, his ass too open for you, and he doesn't care, he lets the world know, *wifey*," she said, sarcastically and we both laughed.

For a couple more hours, I kicked it with my girls and slowly, everyone parted ways.

I had to go in my office and count my money, drunk and all, I didn't miss a beat. I had three of my guards follow me upstairs to guard the door and I went straight to work. After forty minutes of counting, there was a knock at my door. I figured it could only be three people.

When I got up to opened it, Que barged in like he owned the place. He roughly pushed me on my desk and raised my dress up, sliding my panties off. He reeked of liquor but I knew he wasn't drunk because he didn't drink much on a work night. As mad as I was, I couldn't front, the way he shoved me around and fingered my pussy had me moaning in ecstasy.

He pulled out his thick dick and slid it in me, going deep. He kissed me like we were in love. I was so drunk that I didn't even realize this nigga wasn't wearing a condom.

"Que, put a condom on," I said in between moans.

"Nah, ma, you gone have my baby."

"Boy, you know damn well I'm not fucking with you like that."

He pumped harder and faster, shutting me up. I couldn't front, he knew just how I liked it and exactly where my spot was.

"Oooh, Que, I'm about to cum, baby, I'm bout to cum."

"Cum for me, ma."

"Oooh shit, Que."

"Right there, huh? Right there?"

"Yeah, baby, right there! Oh my God, don't stop! yesss right there."

"Ahhh shit!" he growled, that only meant he was cuming with me.

We both laid there breathing hard, trying to catch our breath. That's when we heard the commotion. We looked on the camera that was pointing to the dance floor and it was a stampede of people running. I slid my panties on as he hurried to buckle his pants. We grabbed our straps and ran out the door towards the commotion.

As I was running, my legs felt like they were ready to give out on me, but I was in full gangsta mode, ready to blow a hole in a muthafucka.

When we got to the dance floor, Blaze and Capri were the first two niggas I seen stomping a guy out. Another guy was running towards him with a gun out and my killer instinct kicked in. I fired three shots in his direction, laying him down immediately. That's when everybody looked his way in awe.

"Get every last fucking guard right here, now!" I shouted.

By this time, the club was empty and I needed every guard in attendance. I wanted to know how the fuck did these niggas get in here with guns. My security was on point so somebody had to answer to this shit.

When I had everybody in a circle, I spoke at the top of my lungs to make sure I was heard clearly.

"Who was working the door?" I said in a rage.

Everybody was quiet, and by the way they were looking, I could tell nobody wanted to speak up.

"Me and Cujo, Cash," Larry, my security, spoke up.

"Larry, how the fuck them niggas get in here with guns?"

"I don't know, Cash, but Cujo did the patting and I checked ID's."

I looked over at Cujo and before I could say anything, Que fired two shots into his chest and he instantly hit the ground.

"Damn, Que!" I said, giving him a long stare.

"Fuck all that, ma. That nigga fucked up and ain't no room for errors," he said and stood his ground.

Que was right, we couldn't take any chances and this one was a big ass fuck up.

"Capri, call the Body Boyz, tell them to come clean this shit up, ASAP. Larry, you stay behind until they get here, and everybody else, go before the time come."

Blaze, Que, and I went out the back door to our rides and they followed me home, making sure I got there safe.

We all went inside and had a round table at my kitchen counter because I needed to know what the fuck happened.

"It was them niggas that were all in your face, Cash. He bucked up on me. So, me and Kellz start beating his ass. His homies ran up on us, then all the guards came out of nowhere, so we stomped their ass out. Thanks, Cash, you saved a nigga life, though."

"No problem, Blaze, you know I'll die for you, nigga," I said, and meant every word I said.

Blaze had saved my life many times and I owed him my life. He had my back and I had his front, that's exactly how it's been since day one.

31

My phone rang and when I looked down at it, it was Larry, so I quickly answered.

"Hello?"

"Ms. Cash, the Body Boyz are here."

"Ok, Larry. Did the one-time's come?"

"No, and if they do, the whole place is closed up so they won't get in."

"Ok… well, hit me when the Boyz finish, I'm going to stay up and wait for your call. Be safe."

"Ok, I'll hit you soon."

"One."

"One."

Blaze went upstairs and crashed in his usual room. So, Que and I went into the living room to watch TV. I was tired as a muthafucka and had to meet up with Esco tomorrow. Therefore, the boys stayed with me so we could make our move, first thing in the morning.

My phone rang and it was Quan sexy ass. Quan was my freak daddy who knew exactly what it was. He knew he was a _fuck_, nothing more, nothing less. He didn't pressure me into being his girl, having his baby or falling in love. We fucked and he went about his business and anytime we called each other, it was all about a booty call.

Que was grilling me with his eyes, so I kept my head straight like I was focused on the TV. I made a mental note to hit Quan up in two days because tomorrow I had to re-up and cook. I didn't have time for shit else.

Que's phone rang and by the way he looked, it let me know it was a bitch, but he sent it to voicemail. His phone rang again, so he looked at me and answered it. I turned my head, letting him know I wasn't fazed and he put it on speaker so I could hear their conversation.

"Where the fuck you at?" I heard a woman's voice shouting through the phone.

"First off, bitch, you not my bitch, so why the fuck you questioning me?"

"Whatever, Que, where the fuck you at?"

He shook his head before answering. I could tell he was annoyed.

"I'm at Cash's house since you wanna know so fucking bad."

The girl smacked her lips. "Why the fuck you at that bitch's house? I know yall fucking, you think I'm dumb?"

"Check this out, hoe! Let me ever hear you call her a bitch and I'm going to beat your ass till I see blood," Que said. He was shouting at the top of his lungs.

No lie, it made me feel great to know he would go to the bat for me.

The girl got quiet like she knew he wasn't playing and smacked her lips again.

I chuckled a little bit and he shot me a look letting me know that shit wasn't funny. I rolled my eyes at his ass and turned to look back at the TV.

"You always taking up for her," she shouted, sounding like she was crying.

"So fucking what! Cash is my right hand, and you or no other bitch can come before her, and you know that, Keisha!"

"So I guess she comes before our baby too, huh?" she said, crying even harder.

"Man, come on with that shit, I told you I'm not claiming shit but my money counter. You know damn well you ain't no saint. You be out here fucking everything moving."

"I'm not fucking anybody other than you. I don't want anybody but you, Que. I wish you would get that through that thick ass head of yours."

Before he could reply, I snatched his phone out his hand and ran towards the kitchen, full speed.

"Bitch, didn't I tell you he would be in my bed tonight, hoe? So why the fuck is you calling?"

Before I could finish, he tackled me to the ground. He dropped the phone trying to fight with me. I couldn't stop laughing at what was going on.

After about fifteen minutes of us tussling, we heard her voice say hello through the phone. We both laughed because all this time the dumb bitch was still holding on. He picked it up off the ground and hung it up. He helped me off the ground and we went back to the couch to finish watching TV.

This dumb hoe called back to back and every time, he sent her dizzy ass to voicemail.

"You better answer your phone before your wife fucks you up," I laughed.

"Stop playing with me, Cash, before I fuck you up. You are my only Wifey, I wish you stop playing and make this shit official."

I didn't even reply, I just looked at him and admired his sexy ass.

He thought he was slick, smiling so his dimples would show because he knew that shit turned me on.

Que was fine as fuck and he looked sexy as hell in his briefs and wife beater. His body was right, but it was something about him that wouldn't let me go there.

Deep down inside, I knew me and Que would make the perfect couple. We'd be each other's ride and die. However, I couldn't trust him. He had bitches flocking left and right. In all honesty, I loved being single and not having to answer to nobody. Que was already a jealous ass nigga, so I could only imagine if we were really together how he'd act.

Chapter 3

I woke up to the smell of bacon. I rubbed my eyes, trying to adjust my vision and lifted up off the couch. I headed towards the kitchen. Que was standing over the stove, and Blaze was sitting at the table, drinking a cup of straight black coffee. I don't know how he drank that shit, but he did.

"Morning, uglies," I said to the guys. I took a seat across from Blaze.

"Morning, ma," Blaze said, not taking his eyes off his newspaper.

"Morning, Wifey," Que said, smiling from over the stove.

"Que, you got it smelling good. Keep it up and I'm going to make you Wifey, for real."

"Shut yo ass up, Cash, you ain't wifing shit but your duffle bag," Que responded with his lips curled up.

"And you know it!" I smirked.

He just looked at me and shook his head.

After we ate, I went upstairs to jump in the shower. It was 8:26 am, so I took my time around my room.

Gutta was laying across my bed like she owned the place. I couldn't help but admire her cute little self. She was white, fluffy, and her pink diamond collar made her eyes light up. Everybody said I was crazy because I spent $25,000 on her collar, but what they didn't know was she was very sentimental to me.

I had got Gutta from the only guy I almost fell in love with years ago. I never told him I loved him, but truth be told, I did. He did any and everything for me, but I fucked him over in a major way. His name was Carter and he was the real meaning of a D-Boy. That nigga had an empire like Nino Brown, but with a very good heart.

When my mom got knocked, he helped pick up the pieces of a lost little girl. He taught me how to cook work better than I knew already, and even gave me a piece of one of his territories.

We were inseparable, but for some reason, I just couldn't commit.

One night, he walked in *Cozy's,* a Cuban restaurant on the beach, he had taken me to many of times. I was with this nigga name Carlos. I having dinner when he walked in with his boys. His right hand nodded in my direction, letting him know I was there. When he looked at me, he shook his head in disgust. I felt like shit, no lie. By the look on his face, I could tell he wasn't only embarrassed, he was hurt. We had just gone out the day before when he surprised me with Gutta. He always called me his Gutta

Baby so that's why I named her Gutta. Now, here I was, one day later, fucking up already.

I called him for four days straight, even popping up at his traps, but he never answered. They always said he didn't want to see me. Two weeks later, his little sister had called me and told me he had gotten killed. I really felt like shit. I buried myself in my room for days and cried until I was tired of crying.

At the funeral, his whole life was exposed. He had a wife and family ducked off, and never mentioned it to me. But I didn't give a fuck, we were together all day every day and everybody around him knew I was his Boss Bitch.

To this day, on my end, nobody ever knew that I'd fallen in love, only Malina, and I planned on keeping it like that.

"Come on, Cash. Esco just called," Que said, breaking me out my thought.

"Huh? Oh, ok, here I come."

"You straight, ma."

"Yeah, Que, I'm fine," I said got up off the bed.

I kissed Gutta on the top of her head and made my way to the restroom.

After I showered and brushed my teeth, I went into my walk in closet, took a seat on my throw chair, and looked through my clothes. I settled on some black skinnies, a white baby tee, a black blazer, and some Louboutin pumps. I kept my jewelry simple, rocking my little Jesus piece and diamond tennis bracelet. I threw on my Jesus piece stud earrings and ran my fingers through my loose curls, letting it hang long down my shoulders.

When I looked up, Que was standing behind me, smiling.

"What? Damn, Que."

He laughed. "Nothing, ma. You just sexy as a muthafucka, that's all," he said and walked back out the room.

I grabbed my black and red Louis Vuitton bag to match my Louboutin's and headed out the door right behind Que.

Everybody were in separate cars and by the looks of things, you could tell my crew was eating. Que was driving his Bugatti, Blaze was in his Spider, and I chose the droptop two-door baby pink Bentley because after I handled my business, I was going for a spin out in the town. I slid on my Louis Vuitton shades, my Meek Mill Dream Chasers CD, and headed towards the highway with my niggas in tow.

When we pulled up, we were let right in. We walked through the large home, finding our way to Esco's business room and took a seat. I noticed less duffle bags on the floor beside his desk. I was puzzled, so I spoke first.

"Esco, what's up, Papi?" I said in a flirtatious tone, but I was on some business shit.

"Cash, what's up, my doll. Again, I apologize for what happened. Here are your goods."

"It's cool, Sco, but why so little bags?" I asked with a puzzled look on my face.

"I only have nineteen, Mamacita, Nino come and buy two hundred," he said in his broken accent.

"Come on, Esco, pull my other bricks out yo culo, muthafucka. This aint enough."

"I'm sorry, Cash. I wait for Miguel to bring more, call me later. Nino take too much," Eso said in his broken English.

I was beginning to fume.

"What the fuck am I going to do with 19 bricks? I have split it up between five traps," I thought to myself, but I didn't put up a fuss.

What was really pissing me off, though, was this nigga kept saying the name Nino like I knew who the fuck he was. Fuck Nino! I needed my work. I held my composure, paid my dough, and left with my niggas.

After dealing with Sco's bullshit and Que reassuring me that we will have more work tomorrow, I parted ways with the guys and headed up to the shop to to collect my money. It was a crazy night at the club last night, so I prayed Trap Gyrl's was running smoothly.

When I walked in, it was packed and all the girls were at their work stations with a client in each seat. I went to the back to speak to Nikki so I could find out when was Niya's graduation.

After I hollered at Nik, she informed me It was in three months. I couldn't wait, I had the best gift in store for Niy, and I was sure she would love it.

I went to my office and trapped myself inside for hours. A nap was much needed because tonight I was going to The Cave to cook and it was going to be a long night's process.

The Cave was one of the safe houses that only had a 70-inch plasma, a black leather couch, and six stoves in the kitchen. Que and I would cook, plus our other four hired helpers would cook as well. Some days, I would cook at home, but when it was more than I could handle, The Cave is where it went down. At that moment, I got a text from Quan.

Quan: Sup, sweet thang? I miss you!

Me: Is that right? You miss me or you miss this sweet pussy?

Quan: Both, lol.

Me: Lol, nigga, stop fronting. I'll see you tomorrow morning for a daily dose of that fire ass dick.

Quan: lol, aight, hit me, sweet thang.

Me: *kissy face. *

After texting with Quan, I got comfy on my red leather couch and snuggled myself into a deep sleep. It seemed as right when I was in a good sleep, I heard arguing, so I jumped up. I had to have been sleep for a couple hours because I had occupational hazard. I grabbed Dolly out my purse and went into the shop.

When I stepped into the salon area, two chicks were arguing. A light skin girl who was in Kimmy's chair getting her side shaved was arguing with a dark skin girl who had on a cap and cape, so I assumed she was getting her hair done by Nikki. The girl in the cape was hovering over the girl in Kimmy's chair, screaming about some nigga named Franky B. This shit had me laughing because Franky was one of my jump offs who sold major weed up north. His dick was little as fuck, but he was nice and a super trick. He had babies all over the city and here it was, these hoes were in my shop with they shenanigans.

"Can y'all take that outside, please?" I said in the calmest voice because I was still tired and didn't feel like this bullshit. "Who the fuck are you? And, mind your fucking business," the bitch in the cape, said.

The shop got silent, but I heard someone say *uuh ooh.* I walked right up on that hoe and smacked the taste out the bitch mouth. She squared up like she wanted to rumble, but fuck that, wasn't no fucking fighting today. I pulled out Dolly and hit that bitch upside her head repeatedly until I felt somebody grab me. Ol girl was screaming like she was dying while the other bitch held her mouth open in disbelief.

"Bitch, get the fuck out my shop, hoe!! I bet not ever see you around this muthafucka!"

Nikki ran over and helped her out the door, but I didn't give a fuck or feel any sympathy for the bitch. I didn't say anything to the other chick because I didn't know if she was scared or respectful because the entire time, she remained calm.

I took a seat to calm my nerves and noticed Mo smiling all up in a niggas face while she was re twisting his dreads. I couldn't see the guys face because he was facing her and I wasn't trying to be all in his grill. However, what I did notice was his Giuseppe shoes and iced out watch.

"Yo ass is crazy, Cash!" Nikki said while laughing and walking back through the door.

"Girl, I'm tired and the bitch needs to know who she popping off at the mouth too. This my fucking establishment. Ain't no hoe gonna come in my shit with her extras," I said and looked at her arch enemy.

I looked over at Mo and she was laughing hard as hell. She spun the chair around and ol boy stood up and fixed his clothing. We locked eyes for what seemed like forever until Mo jumped in front of him, kissing him on the cheek. He backed up like he didn't want her to kiss him.

Then it hit me, *"That's the same nigga that was at Esco house the night he sold me some bad work,"* I thought to myself as he walked towards the door. He made sure he glanced over at me one more time.

Mo must have caught it because she looked pissed. She then stormed out behind him. Through the picture window, I could see them in the front, arguing. By the way she was popping her neck and had her hand on her hip, I could tell she was giving him the 3rd degree, but he looked like he wasn't trying to hear any of that shit. Apparently, he wasn't because he walked away, leaving her standing there. That shit made her even more pissed because she stormed back in and headed towards the back, not saying shit to anybody.

My phone rang and the Nicki Minaj ringtone let me know it was Que, which meant it was time to work.

"Wifey, what's up, you ready?"

"Yeah, I'm going to go home and park, you gone come get me?"

"Yo ass don't never like driving," he laughed.

"I'll be there soon so take your ass home."

"A'ight, I'm on my way out the door now," I hung up.

When I made it home, I went upstairs to find Gutta so I could feed her. After I fed Gutta, I took me a quick shower. I suited up in my Adidas tights, a shirt to match, and my pink Adidas tennis shoes. Que let himself in with the spare key he had and found me prancing in the mirror. When I turned around, he was smiling ear to ear and licking his lips.

"What nigga? Boo!" I smiled.

"Come on, ma, yo ass should have been ready."

"Damn, I couldn't wash my ass."

"Hell yeah, wash that muthafucka, I'm sure you smell like another nigga."

"Boy, shut up, I've been at the shop all day."

I then began telling him about my adventure with me going upside a bitch head. We headed out the house. I stopped to hit the alarm on the way out.

"Ms. Lopez," Pedro was calling my name so I stopped before closing the front door.

"Hey, Pedro?"

"That guy came by again, he left you a note," Pedro said while handing me a piece of paper.

All I could do was shake my head.

"What guy?" I asked.

"The guy that pop up the other day."

"Oh, ok," I said in a nonchalant tone.

Que ass was grilling me so I knew I was about to hear it the minute we got in the car.

"Thanks, Pedro. We're going to the cave so I'll see you later."

"Ok, be safe. Call me if you need me."

"I will… I love you, bye," I said and kissed him on the cheek.

When we got in Que's whip, I buckled up and laid back. I then scrolled thru my Facebook timeline. I could see Que giving me his death eyes but I tried to ignore his ass. I don't know why he didn't get the fact that I didn't have to explain shit to him. I knew he was only looking out for me, but at the same time, he acted off of his emotions. I don't know how many times I had to remind this nigga I wasn't his bitch. He was too crazy, straight up.

"So, who is he?"

"Who is who?"

"The nigga that popped up to yo fucking crib, Cash!"

"He ain't nobody," I said, not taking my eyes off my phone.

"So, he knows where the fuck you stay, but he ain't nobody?" He was angry so he started shaking his head.

"His name is Ricky, and like I said, he ain't nobody, Que."

"So, Cash, why the fuck does this nigga know where the fuck you lay yo head? You bugging, ma."

I sighed. I wasn't in the mood to get into it with Que over a nigga I didn't care about.

"Why the fuck you didn't take him to yo little secret hide out?" he asked with a smirk.

I didn't even respond because that shit caught me off guard. Nobody knew about my other house I had, but Pedro and that muthafucka was ducked off in the cut.

"Yeah, why you so quiet? What you thought, a nigga didn't know? Yeah, I been knew about that house."

"What the fuck, Que! Are you following me or something?" I was mad as fuck.

"Something like that." He smiled but wasn't shit funny.

"Ain't shit funny," I shook my head.

"Look, ma, you gotta understand, this the life you chose and if it's one thing I promised to Ms. Lopez was that I would always keep you safe. If I fail her, it's like I failed myself," he said, sounding as sincere as he could.

Everything he said was true. This was the life I chose and I knew at any giving moment, niggas would test me because I was a female. One thing they didn't know about me was I was cut from a cold cloth and there wasn't a scared bone in my body. I'd lay a muthafucka down on instinct. I didn't get this far for being a girl, I'm a gangsta ass bitch with a fucking empire. I had a team of solid niggas and the minute I was tested, they rested!

Chapter 4

When we pulled up to the cave, everybody's car was there, so we got out and walked towards the driveway.

I grabbed Que's hand so he could stop walking and face me. I had a few things to say and it was a perfect time.

"Thank you."

"Thank me? For what, ma?" He looked me straight in my eyes. This nigga was so sexy, I couldn't do shit but smile.

"For everything, Que, I appreciate everything you do for me. I'd die if I ever lost you," I put my head down.

 he grabbed my chin lifting it up.

"You're welcome, ma," he smiled. He then pulled my hand and I followed.

When we got inside, I spoke to the two lady cooks, then the guy cooks.

Arcelie, one of the female cooks, smiled at Que. The look he gave her back let me know something was up. These muthafuckas weren't slick so I made a mental note to pay close attention to their asses.

We threw on our aprons. We then bust down the first six bricks and everybody took their positions in front of a stove. I could have paid six cooks instead of four, but my whip game was on point. Therefore, I chose to help out a little, some days doing it on my own. My mother had the best dope in town because she whipped it herself and at a young age, she showed me the game and I had this shit down to a science.

Every chance I got, I peeked over at Que, then Arceliel. I noticed they kept making eye contact. I wasn't the jealous type and Que had never disrespected me, but that nigga's dick had a mind of its own. This bitch Arcelie knew me and Que were fucking. Shit, everybody in the circle knew it, so sneaking and geeking was out.

"This nigga wanted to play, I could play the game with him," I thought to myself,

Only thing was, I played it better because Que couldn't handle the shit I dished out.

Soon as I was finished the product I had on the stove, I removed it so it can dry and get hard. I walked over to Dre, one of the cooks, and stood in front of him.

"Let me show you a little something-something, Dre," I said in a flirtatious tone, standing in front of him.

He positioned his big frame right behind me to where his dick was literally touching the crack of my ass. I then put my hand on his hand and helped him stir the contents inside the jar, but putting an extra shake in my body movements.

"Damn!" Dre said getting his rocks off and this was exactly the reaction I needed.

"Yeah, you like that, huh? I'm sharp in this department," I said again, being flirtatious.

"Hell yeah, you sharp, ma."

We both started laughing.

Que turned around and the facial expression he had was priceless. He turned his head like he wasn't fazed, so I continued taunting Dre. He was loving every moment of it.

Dre was cute just not my type, but Que jealous ass didn't care, he would accuse me of a blind man in a wheelchair. I played close attention as he sat the jar beside him, then turned around to walk our way. Right then, I knew he couldn't take anymore.

"Get yo shit split, Cash," Que said walking up on us.

"What the fuck is your problem?"

"Man, back the fuck up off her before I put some hot lead in yo ass, Dre."

Dre threw his hands up in the air and stepped back like he didn't want any parts.

"Yo, you bugging, Que," I laughed and walked back to my stove.

"Nah, ma, you just being disrespectful and you are going to make me fuck you up."

"I'm being disrespectful? Nigga, you got shit fucked up! But, you and this bitch over here googly eyeing each other and shit, but I'm slick?"

Arcelie dropped her head, I could tell she was nervous.

"Man, what the fuck are you talking about?" Que said in a lower voice and that shit really gave him up.

"Yeah, I bet, nigga! Let me find out."

"Cash, ain't nobody up to shit. Me and Celie ain't rocking like that, you know I'll never disrespect you and fuck on somebody in our circle."

"Que shut the fuck up. Your nasty ass will fuck anything with two fucking legs," I turned my back on him and got back to work.

For the rest of the night, I remained quiet and continued cooking. I also noticed all the fuck faces stopped and that was really confirmation they were fucking on the low.

"Fuck that nigga," I thought to myself.

I then let my mind drift off to the mystery man. I didn't have a name, a location or nothing. All I knew was that he was sexy as fuck and well kept. I knew I was wrong because he was fucking on Mo, but as much as I tried to shake off the thoughts of him, I just couldn't. He reminded me so much of Carter that it was scary. Everything about him was perfect from his dreads to his smile, and his whole swag itself. Baby was a prize possession.

"It would be a tragedy if his dick was wack," I thought to myself and started giggling.

"Are you almost done?" Que asked while walking up on me and fucking up my train of thought.

"Yeah, this the last one."

He nodded his head and went to lay on the sofa.

After I was completely done, I cleaned up my area, washed my hands, and then slid on my jacket.

On our way out the door, I turned around and waved bye to Dre. He chuckled, shaking his head and Que gave me his death look. I just laughed at his ass and kept walking.

     ***

I didn't even realize I had dozed off until Que was screaming my name like he was crazy. It was 4:12 in the morning and I was dog ass tired. When I looked out the window, I noticed we were at Que's house. Nonetheless, I was so tired, I didn't protest about why he didn't take me home. In reality, this was like my 3rd home and it was closer to the Cave than my house. Therefore, this would be where we were crashing tonight.

I went in and headed straight to his fridge for a bottled water. I peeled out my clothes, dropping each piece as I walked through the house towards his bedroom.

For Que's house to have been a bachelor and him being a hardcore nigga, his crib was laid. He had a five bedroom all to himself, and it was decked out, of course, because he let me decorate everything except his man cave. He didn't play when it came to his little punk ass man cave, he decorated it to his liking and I hated that room. There was a sign on the door that read No Women or Cash Allowed, which was so hilarious. Every time I walked back there, I'd crack up, but he was serious as a heart attack. He really didn't allow me in there. It had a wet bar filled with any liquor you could name, a 70-inch plasma, and a stripper pole for when the guys came thru. He had the entire room decked out in black and white, and it looked like the room DMX had on Belly.

When I made it to Que's room, he was laying in the bed, looking up at the ceiling like he had a lot on his mind. I just got in bed and turned my back to him because a conversation with him was like fighting a war with apes.

After about thirty mins of silence, I couldn't take it anymore.

"Que, what's up, pa, what's on your mind?"

"A lot, ma," he responded like he was lost.

"I'm listening…"

"No lie, Cash, this baby shit with this bitch Keisha got a nigga stressed."

"What about it?"

"What if her baby mines? I don't want any kids, and especially by that bitch."

"Well, it's too late for that."

"I know, but man, I keep telling that bitch to get an abortion."

"So, what, Que, you want me to body the bitch?" I laughed, but I was dead ass serious.

"Nah, ma," he laughed. "If it is mine, I'm going to just have to step up to the plate," he sighed.

So for a few minutes, we laid there in silence.

No lie, I didn't want him to have it either. I was so used to it being just us, I couldn't imagine sharing him with a child and not to mention, having to deal with this dizzy bitch. Que was my right-hand man, my fuck buddy, and my best friend. He was the closest thing I had to a father and husband figure.

We were six years apart, but he stepped up to the plate and loved me like no other. He was wise and had been in the game longer than me, so he taught me a lot. When my mom put him on, he was 14 years old, so when it came to the streets, I learned and picked up on a lot from him. At 32 years old, Que was set. This nigga was a millionaire and kept his head above water.

He wrapped his arms around me and to my surprise, he wasn't trying to get deep inside of me, we cuddled up and called it a night.

When I opened my eyes, Que wasn't lying beside me. I looked at the time and it was 10:40. He wasn't in the restroom and I didn't smell breakfast. Therefore, I laid there for a while and then got up to go brush my teeth.

I was freezing cold, so I put on his oversized robe that had "Q" stitched on the back, and headed downstairs. I still didn't see his ass anywhere in sight.

The balcony door was open, so I stepped out to feel the air. When I looked down, Que was in his pool doing laps. I watched his perfect body swim back and forth across the pool and admired every piece of him. He finally looked up and smiled. He motioned his hand for me to get in and I knew what that meant, he wanted me to jump in from the second story. He knew I'd do it because we've done it plenty of times. The first time I ever did it, I was scared shitless, but Que and Blaze bet $10,000 I wouldn't do it so guess what? You damn right I did it.

I took off the robe and stood on the ledge. I had to pump myself up with a one, two, three like always, and then I jumped in, screaming all the way down. I went all the way down 12 feet, coming back up quickly to catch my breath.

"You a bold muthafucka, ma," Que said, swimming my way.

"Damn right, nigga," I said while wiping water from my face.

He came swam up to me and kissed me.

"Que, didn't I tell you to stop kissing me like we go together."

"Shut yo ass up and take this shit off," he said, tugging at my pink lace thong.

I came right up out of it and then wrapped my legs around his waist. In one swift move, he slid his thick dick in me and then used the water to guide me up and down the shaft. He wasn't even hitting it five minutes and already had me moaning and calling his name.

We stayed in the pool for hours, making love then finally got out wrinkled like old people.

We had worked up a major appetite, so we went straight to the kitchen and pulled out a pack of steaks. I hooked us up some steaks, smothered potatoes, eggs, and biscuits.

Que emerged from the back of the house on his cell then reached out to hand it to me.

"Hello?"

"Sup, baby girl?" my mom said through the phone, excited to finally speak to me.

"Oh my God, Hi, mommy," I shouted into the receiver in a cheery voice. why haven't you called?"

"You know I don't like calling the streets much, but I'm fine and I miss you guys."

"Awww, I miss you too."

"So, what's up with you and Que? I know you ain't gave him none."

"Noooo, mommy," I said, giggling. "I ain't nobody messing with him like that."

"Yeah, she is, Ms. Lopez. I stay hittin that thang," Que shouted through the phone while laughing.

I playfully hit him in his arm and frowned at his dumb ass.

"Don't listen to him, mom." I looked over at him and flicked him a fuck you finger.

"Baby girl, you ain't gotta lie. Que has been in love with you since I was on the streets."

"Ugh, mom, change of subject, please," I laughed.

"Speaking of, what's up with your appeal?"

"Well, I got six more years left. If shit works out in my favor, I'll be home in about two years."

"I can't wait!" I squealed like a little girl. "I really miss you."

"Don't get yo hopes up, ma, anything can happen."

"I know," I said in a low tone because I knew it was true.

Anything could happen. Six years isn't that long but damn, it will be a total of 12 years since I seen my mother and I really missed her. At times, I wanted to break down because shit was hard for me being a woman running a million-dollar empire. Yes, I loved my lifestyle but sometimes, I was too overwhelmed with it.

"Aye, baby girl, lemme holla at Que, I gotta go. But, I love you and I'll be calling back soon."

"Ok, I love you more," I passed the phone to Que. I hated when I talked to my mother because I would instantly get sad.

I headed for the living room and on my way out the door, I heard Que ensuring her that he would never let anything happen to me. Other than that, all he kept saying was yes, yes, and yes.

I went and snuggled up on the couch with Que's Raider throw blanket and turned on Netflix. I wanted to watch my all-time favorite movie State Property, but I was in the mood for some comedy and romance so I settled for Two Can Play That Game. No matter how old this movie got, I still loved it, especially looking at Morris sexy ass.

After Que hung up with my mom, he came to the couch and laid beside me. He looked stressed and it seemed like something was up. However, I didn't want to bother with whatever it was. Hell, I was stressed enough.

For the remainder of the day, me and Que chilled and watched TV. Our phones blew up constantly, but we refused to answer. As long as our traps were straight, fuck everything else.

Chapter 5

I was running around my room like a maniac, trying on outfits. I was finally going out with Quan tonight and to my surprise, we weren't just fucking. I guess the nigga must miss me because he wanted to wine and dine me, and you damn right I agreed. We were hitting up a restaurant called The Palmetto Steak House on the beach. I was happy he loved seafood because lobsters were my favorite.

After scrambling through 12 racks of clothing and 664 pairs of shoes, I finally found a black Fendi dress. The top was lace and the skirt attached was leather. I pulled out my Fendi clutch and of course, I had to rock my black Fendi peep-toe stilettos. Tonight, my arm and neck were draped in a total of 465k worth of diamonds. Call me crazy, but yes, I was taking Dolly and making sure she was secure in my clutch.

Quan wanted to pick me up, but I disagreed because I had to go by the Juice after. Therefore, I was gonna tell him I wasn't feeling good and skip a wild night of sex. My pussy was still sore from a week ago when me and Que spent the whole day tucked away fucking like wild bulls. Truth be told, I wasn't into to the double back shit, letting three or four niggas fuck me back to back. One thing I had was some good pussy, and I planned on keeping my shit tight and right.

When I made it to the restaurant, I handed valet my keys and went inside to find Quan. The restaurant was dimly lit and it had a fireplace in the middle of the floor. The ceiling was decked out in crystal chandeliers so the illumination from the fire danced off the crystal, giving the place a sparkly look.

"HI, welcome to Palmetto. Would you like to be seated?" the front desk greeted me.

"Hi, reservations for Calloway."

"Oh yes, Ms. Cash, he's right this way." She walked towards the back where Quan was sitting.

When I reached the table, I stopped and admired him for a moment. He was looking really nice in his Armani suit coat with his white V-neck shirt, and his neck was dripped in diamonds. He smiled the moment he saw me. He stood up to greet me and that alone had me smiling.

"Sup, sexy?"

"Hi, Quan," I gave him a hug.

"You looking good," he said, looking like he wanted to fuck me right here on the table.

"Thank you, you looking good yourself."

"Thanks, baby. So, what you wanna drink?" he said while flagging the waiter over to our table.

"You know me, a double shot of Hennessy."

"I don't know why I asked," he chuckled.

After we got our drinks, we ordered and talked until our meals came. Of course, he asked can we go fuck after, but I told him my next best lie other than I was bleeding, I wasn't feeling good and that shit worked because he didn't put up a fight.

"Excuse me, Quan," I said as I stood up from my chair. "I'm going to go to the restroom and powder."

"Ok, by the time you get back the food should be here."

When I went into the restroom, I went straight to the mirror. I re-applied my gloss, powdered my face, fluffed my curls, and took about ten selfies, posting my cutest one on Instagram.

On my way walking back to the table, I observed Quan talking to two people. He was talking to a male and female, but I continued walking and took my seat across from him.

The minute I noticed who it was I was stunned. It was the mystery guy, and Mo's man friend, but he wasn't here with Mo. He walked in with a light brown skin girl with a long weave. I had to admit, she was a pretty girl.

We locked eyes for so long that Quan and the woman with mystery guy noticed. I took a sip from my glass to break our contact. I could still feel his eyes piercing me.

This piece of specimen in front of me was fine as a muthafucka and he made me feel some type of way. Quan was fine, Que was bomb as fuck, hell, even Ricky stalking ass was the shit, but this man was perfect. He was that nigga and it's like, the more I ran into him, the more I was starting to realize it.

"How are you doing, Ms. Cash?" mystery man said in a sarcastic tone.

I giggled a little, but I prayed I wouldn't give myself away.

"How are you doing, sir?" I replied back in a sarcastic tone. I referred to him as sir because I didn't even know this nigga name.

We both couldn't stop smiling, and I think the girl he was with caught wind of it because she smacked her lips and sighed all in one breath.

Apparently, he didn't give a fuck because he ignored her and began speaking back with Quan.

I started scrolling through my Snapchat to look busy because the more I looked at him, the more I blushed, which meant the more I'd give myself away.

"Man, what are you doing with a crazy chick like her, Quan? She's trouble," Mystery guy said to Quan and they both laughed.

Before Quan could reply, I butted in.

"I'm not crazy, I'm smooth as they come," I blushed.

"Yeah, ok, ma. Smooth, my ass! Not the way you were pistol whipping that chick at your barbershop."

"Oh my God," I laughed, but I was embarrassed. "It wasn't even like that," I squealed like an innocent girl.

"Yeah, ok," he looked at Quan. "Aye, Quan, what you doing tonight, man? We turning Juice up, come through."

Quan looked at me and chuckled.

"Is that right? Yeah, I might come through." Quan knew about me owning Juice, so he looked at me with a smirk before he gave him an official answer.

"Yeah, I'll pull up, my nigga, and fuck with yal."

"A'ight, bet."

Fuck! I cursed myself because I told him I wasn't feeling good, now we would be bumping heads. I kind of felt bad because they knew each other, and I wanted to fuck this nigga brains out.

They shook hands and ol boy and his little date headed for the exit. It was perfect timing because the waiter was on her way towards us with our food.

After Quan and I ate, we parted ways. I was hoping I could go to Juice get my money and leave before them niggas came because nine times out of ten, Que was going to come through and I didn't need all three of them in the same room. All of them were gangstas and that's what I'm afraid of. But, truth be told, I'd body both them niggas if it came to Que.

I reached over to the passenger seat to retrieve my ringing phone and I knew by the tone it could only be Diane, Niya or Tiny.

"Hello?" I answered almost missing the call.

"Oh my God, I'm going to kill em, I'm going to kill him, Cash!"

It was Tiny, but I could barely make out what she was saying because she was crying hysterically.

"What's wrong, ma?"

"Cash, where are you, I'm bout to kill this nigga Mike."

"I'm on my way to Juice, what happened?"

"I went to take the twins to see my mom. I was supposed to stay the night but I wanted to go home. When I got there, I saw a car parked out front so I went in. when I walked in, bitch Mike was fucking some hoe right in our living room," she started crying again.

My mouth dropped from the bomb she just threw at me and instantly, my blood began to boil.

"What the fuck! So, where are you?"

"I'm on my way to take the kids to my mom house. I swear I'm about to kill this nigga!"

"I'm on my way, I'll meet you at your moms."

"Ok," she wept and then she hung up.

It was about to go down. I hated getting in dick and pussy, especially because Mike was one of Que's lieutenants, but this nigga crossed the line. In her fucking house? Now that was foul. Time after time I've told her to leave his ass but you can't tell a bitch in love shit. He had cheated before and instead of her leaving for good, she always went back.

Mike was a chill nigga getting money, and I really respected him because he'd caught plenty bodies for me and he made me plenty dough. He came across all kinds of fly bitches but fuck that, my bitch was fly too and she had more class wrapped around her finger than in a random bitch's entire body.

It's one thing I believed in and that was loyalty. Cheating was a part of disloyalty and that's exactly why I didn't want a nigga because the fear of him or me cheating. I'd be damned if I bodied a nigga over anything other than money. Therefore, I preferred to keep these skeezers at a distance.

Tiny was loyal to the soil, she would give this nigga her last breath and in one dumb move, he ruined it all.

I made a quick U-Turn and hopped back on the highway towards her mother's house. I did a hundred all the way there and arrived in about fifteen minutes.

When I jumped out the car, she was parked in the driveway with her engine off. I walked to the passenger side and jumped in. Tiny wasn't into the street life or guns, she was an ordinary mother who wanted good for herself and kids. Bodying a muthafucka wasn't her forte. Hadn't it been for Mike being a part of the squad, he'd be on the front of a t-shirt next week.

"So, what's up, ma, what you wanna do?"

She began to cry and the moment she did, her phone rang. She ignored it so I was sure it was him.

"So, what you wanna do, Tiny? I know you not gone leave the nigga."

"I just want him to feel the pain I'm feeling, Cash. This shit hurts! I can't believe he did this in my fucking house. Oh my, God, in my fucking house! I've been the best wife I could. I've never disrespected our marriage, I've never done anything to hurt him," she said and started cried hysterically. I

let her vent because I knew she needed to get it out. This was my good friend for years, so her pain was my pain. The whole time she talked and cried, all I could do was shake my head. My heart went out to her and I was going to be in her corner as long as she needed me.

"Follow me," I opened my door to get out and she immediately started her engine.

I went to my car and hopped in, heading straight back towards the highway. I drove about thirty minutes out to the Carlton Hotel so I could stash her for a week. Her kids were with her mom so I knew they were straight.

"Look, you're gonna stay here for a week until we figure something out. I would let you crash at my crib, but that's the first place he will look for you. You take my car and I'm going to take yours, ok?"

"Ok," she replied in a low tone while shaking her head.

"Don't answer your phone for nobody, especially him because knowing that nigga, he might have a tracker on it."

We both giggled. I was happy I could make her smile.

"Ok, Cash. I love you, and thanks."

"You're welcome, ma. You know I'm here for you."

Once I got her settled in, I jumped back in traffic to head to Juice. I needed to get my money because I hadn't been there in four days, so I knew my shit was piled up.

I turned on my Beyoncé CD. Now I was in a fuck nigga mold, so I sang the words, *To the left, To the left. Everything you own is in a box to the left.*

it was twelve o'clock on the nose and this muthafucka was already jumping. I looked on to the stage and Hershey was doing her thang. She must have been on for a minute because she was completely naked. I made it just in time for my girl Juicy to do her thang.

Juicy was a bad bitch with red hair and a fat ass. Her sexy body was covered in tattoos and she made her thang squirt, driving the men crazy. The moment she did that trick, the niggas went wild

69

and dropped so much dough and of course, the more money she made, the club made.

Juice was the most talked about club in the city, from local celebrities to even stars coming from Hollywood. So as long as I had the hottest bitches in my club, my club would ever be a five-star nightclub.

I went to my office to do what I had to do before the madness began with my male friends.

Quan was showing up, I looked forward to Mystery man coming, I just prayed Que didn't show his ass up, which I knew chances of him not coming would be slim to none because he knew I had to come collect.

It's one thing Que hated and that was me dealing with pick-ups alone, so I knew if he knew I was there at any giving moment, he would be showing his crazy ass up.

knock, knock, knock

"Who is it?"

"It's Mike."

I sighed because I wasn't in the mood for his shit right now.

"Come in, Mike."

When he walked in, he looked surprised to seem. He then went and looked in my restroom, and then in my closet.

"You looking for something?" I said with a smirk.

"Man, Cash, I fucked up," he sighed and took a seat.

"Yes you did, Mike. You dumb as a muthafucka."

"I know I feel like shit!"

"You should, nigga, damn! In yal fucking house, nigga?"

"She wasn't supposed to come back."

"Nigga, that don't justify shit! You should have had enough respect to take that shit elsewhere."

"Where is she? I see her car outside, and I searched the entire club."

"She's not here."

"Cash, for real, where's my wife, man?"

"I don't know, nigga. We met up, swapped cars, and she went about her business."

"I'm not stupid, ma. I know you know where she at."

"Nigga, what chu betta hope is she ain't somewhere getting dicked down by the next nigga."

Before he could speak up, Que was walking through the door.

"Damn, this exactly what I needed," I thought to myself.

Mike just shook his head and walked out.

"Damn, what's up with that nigga?"

"Oh, he didn't tell you?"

"Tell me what?"

"His dumb ass got caught fucking in the house."

"By who, Tiny?" he said, sounding shocked.

"Yes!" I said while shaking my head.

"Wow, that nigga wilding," he shook his head. "You ready to make that drop?"

"Yeah, can you give me a minute? I'm going to go check out Juicy's performance."

"Here you go," he laughed. "Man, I'm starting to think you gay, ma," again, he laughed.

"Boy, get fucked up. You know the only bitch I want to fuck is Oprah." I shoved him in his chest and we both laughed.

Chapter 6

I pulled 10k out one of my duffle bags and headed downstairs to the stage. Juicy was up next, so I mingled around a little, saying my hello's to my staff. I did a walk-through to make sure everything was peaches, and then headed back to the stage and made it rain on a stripper name Candy. When Candy left the stage, I was sure she racked up a few thousand. Candy wasn't ugly, just very petite with no ass. She had a pretty face and a nice set of titties, so she worked with what she had and made her money by any means.

The club got pitch black for three seconds, then the stage backdrop displayed the numbers five, four, three, two, and when it got to one, a bomb dropped and out came Juicy's thick ass. The niggas went crazy just off her entrance. She had like a New Year's Y2K blackout type of thing going on and that shit was dope as fuck. Money was falling from the sky and when I looked up, it was Que dropping all $10 bills from the VIP on to the stage.

We locked eyes and he blew me a kiss, but I smacked my lips and waved his ass off. I did giggle a little because it was indeed cute the way he admired me, up until when he started flipping out, then I would always have to put his ass on time out.

I walked closer to the stage, throwing my first stack. Juicy winked at me and headed over to stand, in front of me, doing the splits. Then, she got up and started bouncing her ass all in my face. I playfully smacked it, then threw another stack and stepped back.

A pair of muscular arms wrapped around my waist and right when I was going to protest, Quan whispered in my ear, causing goose bumps down my neck. I smiled flirtatiously, but it was quickly turned into fear because Que was looking down from the top with the coldest mug on his face.

Shit! I cursed myself, looking back up and just like that, he had vanished. I sighed to myself because I was more than sure he was on his way down and with the look he was wearing let me know it was going to be ugly.

"You sure don't look sick to me, ma."

"I drank a Ginger Ale and plus, I had to come check on some things."

"Well, it's good seeing you again. Hopefully, you're leaving with me," he said, then turned towards the stage, throwing a wad of cash.

"I'll be right back, Quan."

"Ok," he replied, but his eyes were focused on Juicy.

I rushed off before Que walked up on us and by the time I
made it through the crowd, I bumped right into him. He grabbed
my arm, but I forcefully snatched away and headed through the
crowd of partygoers, making my way upstairs to VIP.

Que was hot on my heels. I was trying to dodge his ass, but
the faster I walked, the faster he walked. Some bitch stepped in
front of him and stood close enough for their bodies to touch. By
the body language, I could tell it was more than an ordinary hi and
bye. I looked back at the two but quickly walked away because ol
girl had him hemmed up. I could tell he was trying to get away
from her but she wasn't giving up. Now, if I actually gave a fuck, I
would have snatched his ass up, but the bitch could have him,
maybe he would get off my bumper.

Que thought his ass was slick. He used my power in the
streets to make it look like he was concerned, but that was bull
shit. It was this pussy that had that nigga tripping.

When I got to the VIP, Mystery Guy was right next to us in
his own section. Again, we locked eyes and held our stare for what
seemed like an eternity.

"Cash, you know that's illegal?"

I looked over at Blaze, he was laughing.

"What's illegal, Blaze?"

"Reckless eyeballing," he responded again, laughing.

"Shut up, nigga. You know him?" I asked with a mischievous grin.

"Yeah, that's Nino. That nigga moving a lot of weight."

"Oh, is that right?"

When I thought about it, it all came back to me. That was the muthafucka that had bought all the work from Esco. Yeah, that nigga was doing very big thangs and that's exactly what I needed. Que was pushing big weight and that's where it stopped. Wasn't nobody moving weight like us in town, but Blaze had just confirmed it.

"I know you ain't thinking about?" he shook his head. "Que gon kill you and that nigga."

We both laughed.

"Fuck Que! That nigga bomb as fuck, but he fuck with Mo anyway, so?"

"Mo from the shop?"

"Yep."

"Word? that doesn't surprise me. Shit, Mo has fucked with the whole city."

"Shut up, stupid," I laughed hard as fuck.

I was on my slick shit since Que was still MIA and it was perfect. I sent Nino over a bottle of Dom Perignon Rose and sat back in my booth like the boss I was. When Sandy, my waitress, walked up and handed him the bottle, she must have told him it was from me because he looked my way, smiled, and nodded his head. He used his finger to motion for me to come over. After I got over my butterflies, I strutted over in my sexiest walk possible.

I took a seat next to him and his boys left to give us some privacy.

"Thank you for the bottle, ma," he said as he pulled the cork from the bottle. He poured me a glass. He drunk straight from the bottle and even that shit was sexy.

"You're welcome," I said, picking up the glass and taking a sip.

"So, you here with Quan or you a free agent?"
"No, I'm not here with Quan."

He nodded ok, and that was all the confirmation he needed.

"You come here a lot?"

I looked up and was caught off guard by that question. "Umm, yeah sometimes," I said, bashfully.

"That's what's up," he said, taking a sip from the bottle.

"So, are you and Mo serious?" I asked, changing the subject.

"I knew that was coming," he laughed. "Nah, ma, we ain't shit. I ain't even touch that girl."

"Stop lying, you know you hit that."

We both laughed.

"Nah, on everything, I haven't. We just went out a few times, that's it. To be real with you, Lil Mama, I don't stick my dick in any and everything."

"Is that right?" Now I was more impressed than turned on.

Juicy walked into VIP and immediately hugged me. She had done a wardrobe change and was now in a one-piece red G-string bathing suit. Her thigh high boots stopped right above her knees and her black garter belt was full of money. I tried to stand up but she sat down beside us and just started talking.

"Ms. Cash, I'm almost done for the night. Here's my night's house money. I paid the DJ and tipped the bar."

"Ok, hun," I said, taking the money from her. "Girl, you killed it!"

"Thanks, ma. So, you want me to come bartend tomorrow or are you ok?"

"Its fine, you can have the night off as hard as you worked tonight."

We both laughed.

Nino was looking at me with a strange look, and I already knew what it was about. He was about to grill me for not telling him I owned the club. However, it wasn't even like that. I just hated any and everybody in my business.

"Juicy, can you give this gentleman a lap dance?"

She smiled and got up.

He tried to protest, but she was already in his personal space. She freaked the shit out of him, and I was more turned on. I sat back in my seat and we eye fucked each other the entire time. When I saw Que coming, I whispered to Juicy to keep him occupied till I came back and she agreed. I got up and went to our section, but throwing a stack at Nino and Juicy before heading out.

"Cash, I swear it ain't—"

I cut his ass off before he could finish. "Look, Que, just stay the fuck out my business! You always in my shit about every fucking nigga you see, but every time I look up, some alley cat street hoe all in your fucking grill. That shit not cool at all, I'm not your bitch, Que. I do what the fuck I wanna do, from now on! Oh, and FYI, I can take care of my muthafuckin self!" Just like that, I walked out and because he was guilty, he didn't even come after me.

Que and I had made a vow to never disrespect each other in public with any bitch or nigga, but his ass got away with too much and I was tired of hiding my shit. So after today, I was doing me rather he liked it or not.

When I walked back into Nino's section, I sat down beside him, and Juicy got up off his lap to leave. She kissed me on the cheek bye and headed out.

Nino and I got lost in each other's eyes and neither one of us spoke. To be honest, we could have gazed at each other for the rest of the night because his big brown eyes were beautiful. As much as I loved this feeling, I hated the way he was making me feel because no man had ever had this effect on me, except Carter.

He took it upon himself to rub my legs as he spoke and it only made me snuggle closer to him.

"So, you own the place, huh?"

"Yeah, I do," I said in a low tone.

"That's what's up, Lil Mama."

"What's your name if you don't mind me asking?" I jumped straight to it.

"Nino…"

"No, I don't want yo street name that everybody calls you," I said, tilting my head to the side.

"Ha, why is that?"

"Because, I believe when you like someone you're supposed to know the real them, and Nino ain't the real you."

"Oh, so you like me, huh?" he smiled.

"No, I don't."

We both laughed and he playfully shoved me.

From across the club, I could feel eyes shooting me daggers, and when I looked up, Que had that look of death. No lie,

I felt awkward as fuck, so I quickly turned my head to focus back on Nino.

"It's Brooklyn, ma."

"Oh ok, Brooklyn, I like that."

"And, what's yours?"

"Cash…"

"Oh, it's cool for you to sweat me bout my government, but…"

"No, that's really my birth name, you wanna see my ID?"

"Yep!" he laughed.

Right then, Sandy rushed in yelling and by the look she was wearing, something was wrong.

"Ms. Cash, security has your friend's downstairs hemmed up, they were fighting," she said in a panic.

"What the fuck is going on?" I said, giving her a look of confusion.

I jumped up and run to look from the balcony and Brooklyn was right behind me.

There was a circle formed and a lot of commotion.

"Damn man, not tonight," I thought to myself as I pulled dolly from behind my back and held her to my side.

Que and Blaze saw my sudden move and before I knew it, their weapons were drawn and they were ready to move.

When Que ran past us, he mad dogged Nino up and down and proceeded towards the stairs. I followed closely behind him.

Nino must not have noticed or he was too focused on what had transpired because he didn't say shit. He acted on instinct, pulling his gun from his waistline and followed suit. I made a mental note to check my security later because somebody had to answer to why this nigga was in my club strapped up. However, now wasn't time to focus on that because the way he moved, I was able to tell he had my back and riding with the squad.

When we reached the circle, Tiny little ass was in the middle and screaming at the top of her little lungs. Mike was all in her face and he looked heated. Therefore, I rushed to his side to make sure he was straight. I was relieved to see nobody was hurt and it was just these two having marital problems. But hell no, not tonight, in my club and especially while I was trying to get my mack on.

Security was holding Mike back, but because he was a part of my squad, they knew better than to make any wrong moves. I grabbed Mike because I knew nobody but me could calm his crazy ass down.

I motioned for Que to grab Tiny and take her upstairs, and he was already on top of it.

"I'm so sorry, Brooklyn, can you give me a minute," I said to Nino and pulling Mike away from the crowd.

"I'm sorry. Cash, but this bitch foul. She dancing with a nigga and he rubbing all up on her ass and shit like she some cheap hoe," Mike said in frustration.

"Ok, Mike, just calm down."
"Fuck no, I can't calm down, this bitch disrespectful," he said as he punched the wall.

"First off, nigga, you are about to calm the fuck down in my fucking place of business. I don't care about you killing the bitch, but not here and not tonight, nigga!"

He must have seen I was serious because his face softened a bit.

"My bad, ma. Man, she got me hot."

"I understand, Mike, but you the one fucked up first. She just hurt right now and want you to feel her pain. Trust me, she ain't gone fuck none of these niggas. If she wanted to step out on you, nigga, she would have been doing that. Look at how many times you fucked up and she ain't stepped out on you once."

He shook his head, but he agreed to what I was saying.

"Man, Cash, I fucked up."
"Yes, you did, and I don't know what you gon do to fix this shit but you on the verge of losing the best thing that ever happened to you, so fix it fast, Mike!" I stormed off and went to find Brooklyn.

When I found Brooklyn, he was standing at the end of the dance floor. I walked up on him while smiling just to ensure him that everything was ok. I grabbed his hand and lead him through the crowd and back upstairs to VIP.

When we got upstairs, Que had Tiny hemmed up in the corner trying to calm her down. She was still beyond pissed, trying to get to Mike. Tiny's little 5-foot 2-inch frame moved wildly but Que was able to contain her without much force.

"Not tonight, ma. Especially not in my shit!" I said to her the minute I was in her space.

"I'm so sorry, Cash, but this nigga got me twisted. It's over, I'm single, and I'm about to do my thang!" she shouted with tears streaming down her angelic face. Her body language screamed she was drunk, but I couldn't say I didn't blame her actions.

"Tiny, where's my car?"
"At the room. I took a cab so that bitch ass nigga wouldn't see me," she said, rolling her eyes and snapping her neck.

I just shook my head because this shit was going to get uglier by the day, and I saw it coming.

"I'll give you a ride if you need me too," Brooklyn said as he walked up on me.

"You ain't taking her nowhere, homeboy!" Que protested with aggression.

I put my hand up for him to fall the fuck back.

"Que, can you please drop Tiny off?"

He gave me a stern look like he wanted to slap the shit out of me, but the look I gave his ass let him know I wasn't in the mood.

"Yeah, aight!" he said, mugging Brooklyn. He grabbed Tiny's arm, leading her out of the VIP.

"Blaze, make sure Mike is straight and he gets home safe. I'm going to call you tonight when I get home."

"A'ight, Boss Lady," Blaze said. He then gave Brooklyn daps as a thank you and walked out.

Brooklyn and I walked out hand in hand. I nodded to all my staff, letting them know I was straight and we made our way through the crowd.

Everybody went back to partying like normal and we even got a few funny looks because nobody was used to seeing me hand in hand with a guy, other than Que.

When we made it outside, his crew was behind us. He stepped to the side and said a few words to them, and then everyone departed. We hopped in Brooklyn's black Bentley that was parked right in the front.

"I don't know who this nigga think he is, but he sure had too many privileges like he owned the place," I thought to myself and that was something else on my list to holler at my staff about.

I laughed to myself because I liked how he moved. He was like a male version of me and I couldn't understand it, but it was true.

I buckled my seatbelt and we pulled off in silence. I gazed out the window because I didn't know what I was doing, but after tonight, I was more than sure he was going to be around for a very long time.

"So, what's up with you and Que?" Brooklyn asked.

I was so caught off guard by his question, I barely could answer, stumbling over my words. "Ummm, how you know Que?" I asked curiously.

"I don't know him, but I've heard of him. When you from the streets, ma, you gon always know the important people. The nobodies don't get talked about," he said, looking back and forth from me to the road.

He was telling the truth because Que had a name in these streets. His reputation was money, hoes, death, and his name rang bells all over the state.

"Yeah, you're right, but nothing, that's my Chief," I responded to his question, lying through my teeth.

"Is that all, little mama? Because it doesn't look like it."

"That's it, he's my right hand, Brooklyn."

"Yeah, aight." He let the conversation go, but the way he said it, I could tell he didn't believe me.

The rest of the ride was a silent one. This nigga had me on cloud nine like I was twelve years old. Damn, I felt bad for Mo because from the way she was glowing, I could tell he had her wide open. But I did feel a lot better knowing they never had sex. Well, at least that's what he said. I knew Mo was gone trip but that bitch fucked at least three of my nigga's and used the same lame excuse every time… "But, Cash, you're not fucking him."

Mo was easy. So what, I wasn't fucking them because I wasn't into just giving up my pussy, but that didn't mean go behind my back and fuck them all. Had I been one of those types of girls that fought over nigga's, me and Mo would be locking up occasionally. Every nigga she fucked got back to me, but I never tripped because I didn't love these hoes.

Chapter 7

We pulled up to a house that was in an upscale suburban area. I figured it was Brooklyn's because of the fly ass whips parked in the spiral driveway and all the security surrounding the outside. I must admit, I was very impressed with not only his home but the fact that he had brought me here. This nigga didn't know me from a can of paint so it made me feel special.

I stepped out the car, making sure I put an extra strut in my step. My heels clicked the stone pavement as we made our way to the door. My butterflies kicked in, and I couldn't turn back now because he was already punching in his security code to his alarm. When we stepped inside, I was applauded. His home was breathtaking. No lie, he had taste and it made me wonder did he have a wife because it sure had a woman's touch.

"Is this your house?" I asked, already knowing the answer.

"Yeah, you like it?"

"Yeah, it's really nice. Where's your wife?" I chuckled.

"She's in the room."

I looked at him like he was crazy.

"Haha, I'm just playing. No wife, lil mama."

"Is that right, and why is that?"

"Because, I haven't found a woman worthy enough. The wife title is a very big title to hold and these sack chasing bitches don't know how to be a wife, ma," he said in a serious tone and he wasn't lying.

"True that, but can you be a loyal husband?" I smirked.

He kept quiet.

He led me into the foyer and I took a seat on the wheat leather couch as he vanished out of the room. When he got back, he was holding a cup of Cognac in one hand and a wine glass with a bottle of Moet in the other. He sat the glass down and poured me a drink, sliding it across the table in front of me. We drank and talked for what seemed like forever. Our chemistry was beyond crazy, but he wasn't trying to make a move.

He led me upstairs to his bedroom and let me take a shower. At first, I was a bit shy, but when he left the room, leaving me alone, it calmed my nerves. When I finished my shower, I took it upon myself to lay across his bed, and the minute I laid down, Que was calling. I thanked God that Brooklyn wasn't in my presence.

"Hello?"

"Where the fuck you at, Cash?" he asked, yelling into the phone.

"What's up, Que?" I responded in an annoyed tone.

"Cash, don't fucking play with me! You at that nigga house, huh?"

"No, I'm not, Que."

"You a muthafuckin lie! You don't even know that nigga!" he shouted again, sounding like he ready to jump thru the phone and fuck me up.

Brooklyn walked in and stood by the door. He was wearing nothing but some Calvin Klein briefs and his sexy ass chest was bare. This man was beyond gorgeous and he knew exactly what he was doing.

"Ok, Que, I gotta go."

"Bring yo ass home now, Cash! I'm not fucking playing," he hung up on me and the way he sounded, I knew it was about to be trouble. But fuck that, for the 1,000,000 time, Que was not my nigga.

"Should I drop you off?" Brooklyn said, smiling.

"No, I'm fine."

"Are you sure because it sounds like you're in trouble."

"Haha, funny, I'm not in trouble and besides, I'm grown."

"Yeah, ok, ma," he said, taking a seat on the bed next to me.

Brooklyn and I talked till the sun came peeking through the clouds. He was mad cool and I loved his company. We talked about all kinds of things and it surprised me that he had opened up as much as he did.

When I opened my eyes, I looked around while trying to adjust my vision. I had damn near forgotten where I was and when I remembered everything from last night, I smiled. I went in Brooklyn's bathroom and searched his cabinets for a toothbrush. Just my luck, it was a box full of them. I felt kind of jealous because I knew more than likely they were for all his company and of course, his female companions.

After I brushed my teeth and washed the crust from my face, I walked down his long hallway, looking in every room until I found him. He was lying across one of his guest beds, sound asleep. I leaned up against the wall and admired his sexy face structure while he slept peacefully. His long dreads were sprawled over his pillow and his full lips were calling my name. I wanted to kiss him so bad, but I was nervous. Fuck that, I let my courage build up and tried my hand. I walked over to the bed, making sure I was careful not to wake him. I bent down, planting a kiss on his soft lips and he opened his eyes quickly. I could clearly tell he was a light sleeper and I prayed he wouldn't be upset. He smiled and wrapped his arms around me, pulling me down to the bed but on top of him. I was wearing one of his oversized t-shirts with nothing under it, so my pussy was pressed against the bulge in his briefs.

"Good morning, Lil Mama," he said, kissing me on the tip of my nose.

"Good morning, Big Poppa," I responded.

We both laughed.

"How did you sleep?" he asked, brushing a strand of hair out my face. The way he looked at me had me on the edge. It was as if he craved me, and the feelings were mutual.

"I slept great, could've been better if you would have been next to me."

"My bad, I didn't want you to think I was up to something."

"Well, maybe it was good you didn't."

We laughed again.

"So, what are you doing today, Lil Mama? Can I take you to breakfast?"

"Um, I don't know. I have to go home and get dressed, and then I have to go to the shop."

"Word? How long are you gonna be there?"

"I don't know, a few hours maybe. Why? What's up?"

"Shit, just asking. So, could I see you tonight?"

"Sure," I responded in a hurry.

I was happy he asked because I definitely wanted to see more of him. I don't know what it was about this man, but I was crushing hard. One side of me was saying leave him alone before I fall, and the other half of me was saying fuck it, give it a shot and I was going to do just that.

We got up and went to his master bedroom. I slid back into last night's clothing and we headed outside to his ride. As much as I loved his company, I couldn't wait to get home, shower, and change my clothes.

His phone rang and when he answered, he looked worried. He looked at me and motioned with his finger to give him a minute, so I got in and waited patiently. When he finished his call, he came to the passenger and tossed his keys into my lap.

"Cash, take my car, ma. Something went down at one of my traps. I'm going to get with you later, ok?" he said with a very worried look.

"Is everything ok?"

"Man, I don't know. That was one of my workers, he didn't wanna say much over the phone."

"Ok, call me and let me know you're ok."

"I sure will." He kissed me on the forehead.

I got out to hop in the driver seat. If it was one thing I understood was business and when it came to money, it was the number one priority. I just prayed that everything was ok.

The entire ride home, I thought about Brooklyn. Everything about him seemed so perfect. I know it was so soon, but he seemed like somebody I could fall in love with. After last night, he showed me that he had my back, and especially when he didn't try and make a move on me so soon.

When I pulled up to my house, I searched the premises for Pedro until I found him out back playing golf. I took a seat on the bench and waited until he finished hitting the ball, hoping he would finally look up to notice me.

"Cash, what's up, Mi Amor?"

"Hey, Pedro."

"So, I see you have a new love."

I looked at him astonishingly as to how he knew what was up. He looked down at my phone and I smiled because I had forgotten about our tracking device we installed on our iPhones.

"Yeah, I guess you can say that," I smiled at just the thought of having a new love. "Actually, that's what I wanted to talk to you about."

"I'm all yours, talk to me."

The minute he said that I jumped straight into it.

"What do you know about Brooklyn?"

"Brooklyn?" he asked as if he was puzzled.

"Nino..."

"Oh, Nino. He's a cool guy, but very dangerous, Cash. He pushes big weight and has plenty enemies. He has no wife, no kids, and his parents were murdered when he was young. I did lots of work for his dad many, many years ago," Pedro said in his strong accent, referring to hitman jobs.

"Oh, ok."

"He's a good guy, Cash. He actually reminds me of you."

The minute Pedro said that I laughed because I felt the same way. Brooklyn reminded me so much of myself that it was scary.

"I just hope he ain't a dog like me," I thought to myself while laughing.

I knew Pedro would give me the run down because he knew every D-boy in the entire state of Miami, and even did a few hits for a few.

After talking to Pedro for a while, I walked into the house to find Gutta. The part about Brooklyn being a dangerous guy stuck in my head but It didn't matter because I was a dangerous bitch. I ran the same type of operation he did and I had plenty enemies as well. In this game, everybody had enemies because wherever there was a true hustler, there were ten haters lurking and plotting on what you had.

I ran me a nice hot bath and laid on the bed while rubbing Gutta until the tub filled up. Right when I was about to get in, my phone rang, so I lifted up on my forearms and answered.

"Hey, Nikki?"

"Hey, ma, what you doing?"

"Girl, just got home, about to take a bath and come up there."

"Bitch, you are not gonna believe this," she said, sounding like she had juicy gossip.

"Awe shit, what happened now?"

"Girl, Mo was talking to one of her clients, who happened to be my cousin, and the bitch didn't even know while she was running her mouth. She said how she saw you leaving with Nino last night and yal were holding hands."

"Oh wow! So, why the bitch didn't say shit?"

"I don't know, but check this. She called you all types of hoes, and you gon die when I tell you this part."

"Fuck her, but I'm listening…"

"Bitch, she told her how she fucked Que."

"What!" I said, in shock.

Now my blood was boiling. Que knew I didn't play that shit, especially with a carbon copy ass bitch like Mo. Mo secretly hated me, and she didn't know I knew. One of my old niggas, she fucked on, came back and told me everything she said about me. I hated drama and I was not a fan of gossip, but when the bitch told the nigga about my operation, it had me looking at the hoe sideways.

"Yes honey, that bitch is foul. You know I had to tell you."

"Yep, good looking out. But yep, I got something for that hoe that's about to hurt her feelings."

"Awe shit, I'm scared to ask."

"Don't trip, ma. I'm on my way there."

"Ok, see you in a bit," she disconnected the line.

I wanted to call Que's ass so bad but I didn't even sweat it. I figured some funny shit had gone on between the two, I just could never place my fingers on it. I didn't trip, though, I through that piece of info into my memory bank and I was going use it as ammo against his ass.

When I got out the shower, I slipped into some white jeans and a red Fendi crop top. I put on my red thigh high boots and grabbed my red and white Fendi bag to match. I took my Fendi shades out the case, put them on, and was on my way out the door. As tired as I was, I had to be a mean girl, so I hurried and left.

Chapter 8

On my ride to the shop, it seemed like I couldn't get there fast enough. I was doing 80 MPH in Brooklyn's Red Spider, honking at the dumb ass drivers in my way, and I still wasn't getting there fast enough.

I dialed Que's number and to my surprise, he didn't answer. Therefore, I called right back and this time, I was sent to voicemail.

This shit was making me mad because I could have been in trouble and this muthafucka was too busy in his fucking feelings. I made a mental note to hit up the trap after I left the shop because if it's one thing this nigga had, that was me fucked up.

When I pulled up to the shop, I was sure to park right in the front. His tinted windows were dark but I could see Mo looking hard out the picture window trying see was it Brooklyn. When I stepped out, I could see the bitch neck snapping like she seriously had a problem, and that's exactly what I wanted.

When I walked in, I made my rounds and the whole time, I could feel the bitch eyes watching me, but she didn't say shit. I was ready for Mo to pop off because she had a *long time ago* ass whooping coming. Mo was a little scrapper, no lie, but the bitch couldn't fuck with these hands and she knew it just like I knew it.

After Nikki was done with her client, I sashayed over to her station.

"Hey, Cash," she said happily like she hadn't just talked to me.

"Hey, Nikki," I said, giving her a hug.

I sat down in her chair and looked at my reflection in the mirror. "I really wanna try something different with my hair."

"Bitch, I know you are not thinking about cutting it."

"Hell no, girl, this ain't no waiting to exhale moment," I said, and we both laughed.

"Ok, so, what you wanna do?"
"I don't know, maybe some red highlights. I haven't had red in a minute."

"Awe shit, Cash, you must like him?" she said, nudging me in the arm.

"Nooo," I said, laughing. "It ain't him."

"Yeah, ok, whatever you say. Ok, well, I have two hours before my next appointment, let's do it." She wrapped a cape around me.

I heard a male voice ask for Cash and through the mirror, I could see one of my workers pointing in the direction I was sitting. A Caucasian man was walking in my direction holding some all-white roses. I put my hand over my mouth to hide my smile and he walked up on me handing me the roses.

"Are you Cash Lopez?"

"Yes…"

"Ok, sign here for me, ma'am."

I signed and he left as fast as he came.

I could hear chatter throughout the office, which was weird because niggas did this all the time.

"To my surprise, it worked," I thought to myself as I took out the card to read.

You got a nigga on some corny shit. but anything to make you smile, Lil Mama!

Big Poppa.

Once I read the card, I knew exactly who the roses were from.

Brooklyn.

I smiled from ear to ear and Nikki wasn't making it any better. I had to admit, I was loving the little nickname I adopted, and this little stunt he just pulled was working.

"Awe, Cash, they're beautiful," Nikki said while smelling each one like they all would have a different scent.

"They are," I was beaming.

Brooklyn was smart, during our conversation last night, he asked me questions no guy has ever asked like what's my favorite color, my favorite food, and even my favorite song. He was getting major brownie points and not to mention, he didn't give two fucks about Mo even being here, so that let me know that what he said was true.

From across the room, Mo was mugging me but still hadn't said two words to me and I was fine with that. Me and Nik continued my hair as I pulled out my cell and dialed Brooklyn's number.

"Sup, Lil Mama?"

"hey, Big Poppa," I said in a whisper so Nikki couldn't hear me. But the nudge at my shoulder let me know she did just that. I giggled and proceeded with my call, ignoring her mimicking me. "So, I take it everything is ok?"

"Not really, the spot got hit by some small time stick up kid, but I'll tell you more about it in person."

"Ok. I loved the roses, thank you," I said, changing the subject.

"You ain't gotta thank me, ma. I said I want to do anything to make you smile."

"And you did just that," I started to blush.

"I'm glad you like them. So, what you got up?"

"Nothing much, at the shop. Your girl here, she gone fuck you up."

"Ha, I'm talking to my girl on the phone."

"Is that right? So, I'm your girl?"

"Yeah, you Bae," he laughed, but his answer made me melt.

"Aww," I said cheesing from ear to ear. I was sure he heard me giggling through the phone.

"You still in my whip?"

"Yep, I sure am."

He started laughing. "You wild, ma, but that's what's up. Let them bitches know who you belong to."

"Who do I belong to, Brooklyn?"

"As of now, me! And, in due time, you'll see."

"Well, show me because right now, I'm still a free agent," I smirked.

We both laughed.

"Oh, I'm going to show you, alright. So, what's up, can we do dinner tonight?"

"Um yeah, I guess if you're not busy."

"If I was busy, I wouldn't have asked, ma."

"True. Well, what time should I be ready?"

"Shit, you in my car, you tell me what time should I be ready."

"Oh, yeah," I said, and we both laughed again.

My line beeped, and I was annoyed because I didn't want to be interrupted. I was about to let it go to voicemail until I looked and it was Blaze.

"Hey, Brook, I'm going to see you tonight, ok?"

"Aight, ma, see you later," he hung up.

I clicked over.

"Hey, Blaze."

"Cash, get to spot four, right now. Some niggas ran up in it this morning."

"What the fuck! Who was there?"

"Johnny and Young."

"Oh my gosh, are they ok?"

"Yeah, they straight. I just need to holler at you, ASAP."

"Ok, where's Que?"

"I don't know, he ain't been answering all morning."

"Ok, I'm on my way."

"Ok..."

We hung up and Nikki was just about done with my hair.

"Cash, is everything ok?" Nikki asked in a concerned tone.

"Yes, and no, Nik, the spot got hit but everybody straight."

"Well, that's good. Yeah, go and handle your business, if you need me to do anything else just come back."

"Ok thanks, Nikki," I said, reaching in my purse and handing her a crisp hundred.

I did 100 MPH towards the spot, but when I thought of Que stupid ass, I took a detour to that bitch Keisha's house because I figured that's where his ass was. Damn right I knew where the bitch lived. After our altercation in the mall, I had my computer whiz friend, Marcus, give me everything on the bitch from where she lived, her parents lived to even where her son went to school.

When I got there, her car was parked out front and Que's Bentley was in the driveway. I made my way to the door and knocked like I was the police, making sure these muthafuckas would hear me. When she came to the door, the first thing I noticed was her belly poking out and I actually laughed because I thought about me and Que's last conversation about her being pregnant.

"What the fuck are you doing here?"

I pushed right past her ass, going to find Que. Her house was nicely decorated and I was more than sure everything in it was complimentary of Que. I walked down the hallway, pushing open each door and when I reached the room that appeared to be the master bedroom, Que was laid across the bed, asshole naked.

"Que, get your stupid ass up!" I shouted, shaking his ass awake.

"Que, what the fuck is she in my house for?"

"Bitch, keep talking and you won't have a house!"

Que must've heard the commotion and finally woke up. He looked at me strange as if he seen a ghost.

"Cash, what are you doing here?"

"Que, get your bitch out my house!"

I went charging for the hoe, and Que jumped up to stop me. He was holding my arms in the air while I was trying to get that bitch.

"Cash, chill, ma. What's up, why are you here?"

"Nigga, while you laid up with this chicken head hoe, the fucking spot got ran up in!"

"What!" he shouted and began putting on his clothes.

I walked out the room and headed for the car to wait on him. Shortly after, he was coming out. He shook his head because I was in Brooklyn's car, but he knew right now was not the time to be on no dick and pussy bullshit.

He hopped in and the ride to the trap was a silent one.

I took it as my que to play this song I wanted him to hear. Therefore, I reached for the volume, turned it up, and laid back in my seat.

As the sounds of Party Next Door "Recognize," boomed through the speakers, I prayed he was carefully listening and understanding every word. I loved this song and it reminded me so much of me and Que because he had bitches, I had niggas, and I wasn't tripping at all. He remained silent, I could tell he was in deep thought listening to the words, so when it went off, I played it one more time, hoping he'd catch my drift.

When we pulled up to the spot, the whole crew was there, so we hurried in to see what was going on.

"I need everybody at the safe house, now!" I said, the minute I walked in. It wasn't safe having a meeting at any of the traps because any giving moment anything could happen.

There were all kinds of foreign cars parked out front and that was not good for business. Everybody got up and went to their cars. I made Young ride with me so he could fill me in on everything that happened.

"Ms. Cash, it was that nigga you used to fuck with," Young said the minute he got in the car.

"Who, Young?"

"I don't know his name but he drives that new red Camaro," he said, stuttering.

That's when it hit me. "Ricky?"

"Yeah, I think that's his name," he said, shaking his head yes at the same time.

All I could do was shake my head because I knew Young wasn't lying. I mean, why would he say Ricky, out of all people? Ricky was a snake nigga. The only thing was, I never thought he'd snake me.

Ricky and I had been knowing each other for a long time. I knew he was a stick-up kid, but he showed me I could trust him. This nigga even knew where I laid my head. I wasn't worried about that, though. I had more than armed security around my house. Nobody, but Que, knew I had a sharpshooter on the roof 24/7 and the minute anything looked funny, he was bussing first and asking questions later. Not to mention, Pedro and all my other guards were ready for whatever. Ricky didn't have the balls and if he did, he wouldn't make it past the front gate alive.

"What kind of car was he driving, Young?"

"He was in a black Crown Vic with dark ass tint."

"Ok." I then focused on the road.

Blaze and Que were in the car right behind me. Since Que was still acting like a hoe, he chose not to ride with me. But, I didn't give a fuck, I was trying to get to the bottom of this shit so I could go lay up and ease my mind.

When we pulled up to the safe house, everybody went straight to the roundtable and took a seat. I took my seat at the head of the table like always, and Que sat on the opposite side of me as normal. I found it ironic how my trap and Brooklyn's trap both were hit at the same time and while everybody was clubbing at Juice. Now, I didn't know if Ricky was watching us or if we had a snake in the crew, but I was surely going to get to the bottom of this shit, fast. I pulled out my phone to call Brook and he answered on the second ring.

"Hey?"

"Sup, ma? You ready already?"

"No, not yet," I smiled.

Que was evil eyeing me, so I got to the point. "Where are you?"

"I'm on Darby Ave right now, about to head home and get ready." That was music to my ears because Darby Ave was ten minutes away from the safe house.

"Pull up on me, I need to holler at you ASAP. It's about your trap."

"Aight, say no more. Where you at?"

I gave him the address and we sat patiently, waiting for him to arrive.

When Brooklyn finally arrived, Que stood up and mad dogged him. However, I put my hand up to let him know right now was not the time. He sat back down with a real fucking attitude.

Brooklyn walked over and kissed me on the forehead and everybody looked at Que. I just dropped my head embarrassed. He then walked over to the middle of the table and leaned up against the wall.

"Everybody, this is Nino. He moves weight on the North and East of the city. Pretty much everything we are not touching," I then smirked at Brook and he laughed. "Nino's trap got hit last night too and I'm sure it was connected."

"Yeah, I heard of you. You be doing big thangs," Young said, giving him dap.

Que grilled his ass, so he immediately shut up and sat back down.

"Brook, what kind of car them niggas was in that hit your spot?"

"A black Crown Vic with tint."

I nodded my head because I already figured that was the car.

"Young said it was Ricky."

"What, Ricky?" Koby, one of my soldiers, asked. He was shocked to hear it was Ricky.

"Her little boyfriend Ricky," Que said. He looked at Koby and then looked at Nino with a smirk.

I shook my head in disgust. Que was on some real weird shit.

"Ricky from Gary Projects, Koby," I said to Koby and then gazed at Brook.

"So, what he want from me, Cash? What, is he mad that you are my girl now or something?" Nino said while looking at Que with the same smirk.

"These niggas are tripping," I thought to myself. Don't get me wrong, it was kinda cute, but I felt uncomfortable as hell.

"I don't know, Brook, but what I do know is he's a stick-up kid and this is what he does for a living. The nigga dabbled in a little dope but nothing major. Last night he could have possibly known we were all out at the club so it was a perfect time for him to make his move."

"That's crazy," Brook said, leaning off the wall. "Just point me to the little nigga, Cash, I'm going to body his ass myself," Brook said. I'm sure he meant every word we had spoken.

I ignored him and focused on Johnny.

"Johnny, how did this nigga get in my trap?"

This nigga looked spooked and my question caught him off guard.

"I don't know, Ms. Cash," he was stuttering.

"How you don't know and you were downstairs with some bitches when them niggas came in?" Now I was getting mad because something was up with this nigga.

"Blaze, get this nigga phone," I said while looking at Blaze, and he did what he was told.

Blaze went right into his pockets, retrieved his phone, and tossed it to me. I opened my phone and went to Ricky's phone number in my contacts. I opened Johnny's phone and the shit stared me dead in the eyes. The un stored number in Johnny's phone was the same exact number I had stored for Ricky. It was all adding up, this nigga Johnny had set us up.

I got up and went over to Que, taking his gun from his waistband and walked up on Johnny. He started trying to plead his case, but there was no explanation. He was a snake and we couldn't chance it. Therefore, I lifted up the gun, aimed it at his head, and pulled the trigger. His head burst open like a watermelon and his body fell straight to the ground. All I could do was shake my head at this piece of shit nigga laying in front me. I took that hoe ass nigga in when he was literally sleeping in cars and this was the muthafuckin thanks I got.

"Blaze, call the Body Boyz, get this shit cleaned up, please?" I looked over to Young. "Nigga, you gone pay up for every single brick these niggas took from my spot."

"I got you, Ms. Cash," Young quickly responded because he didn't want to end up like Johnny.

Young was 19 years old, but a true diehard soldier. He was a killer at heart and just like me. He was forced into this life but it turned out to be an adrenaline rush for him just as well as myself.

"Somebody need to find this nigga Ricky and take him to the chambers ASAP. Call me the minute you get a hold of him. Marcus has all the info you'll need to every location he would ever be, even his son's doctor's office," I walked towards Brooklyn. I grabbed his hand and Blaze walked up to dap him.

Que grabbed my arm very aggressively. I just thanked God Brook and Blaze had walked out to talk. I was very anxious to hear what this nigga had to say, so I tapped my foot, looked at my Rolex watch so he could see he had about three minutes.

"Did you fuck him, Cash?"

I just looked at Que and shook my head. I knew he loved me but right now, he was looking weak and this wasn't the Que I knew.

"Why, Que?"

"Just answer the question, Cash!" he shouted.

I looked at him and read his eyes. I could tell he was hurt but fuck that, he had skeletons that I could never forgive, so I hit him with the ultimate.

"Why the fuck does it matter, Que?"

"Because it does, now answer the question."

"You know you got some fucking nerves, Que. You are always trying rain on my parade but all the undercover shit you do I let ride," I said while shaking my head.

"I don't do shit, ma."

112

"Oh yeah, so I guess fucking Mo ain't shit, huh?"

He looked at me stuck on stupid. I knew he was curious to know how I knew but right now, it didn't matter. I just shook my head, snatched my arm away, and walked out leaving him standing there.

When I made it outside, Blaze and Brook was still talking, so I walked past them, trying not to interrupt their conversation. Brooklyn grabbed me by my waist and pulled me close to him. The look Blaze was giving me was a look that said Cash is in love, finally.

"You betta take good care of her, Nino," Blaze said. He was serious but he was laughing as well.

"You got my word, Blaze," Brook replied.

They gave each other daps. Blaze jumped in his ride and pulled off.

"You look tired, ma. Let's go home."

"Home? And where's that?"

"Girl, you know where home is at. Now, come on, follow me."

I didn't protest, I did what I was told. I hopped in his Spider while he hopped in his Aston Martin and we pulled off.

Looking back, I could see Que getting in his car. He looked like he just lost his best friend and in reality, he did. I felt fucked up inside because just a week ago, we were on to something that seemed different. Just a week ago, nothing could come between us and just a week ago, I was nestled in his arms. I felt myself getting closer to Brooklyn and further away from Que, but it was now time we lived our lives.

The only thing missing in my life was real love. As bad as I didn't want to be in a relationship, being with Brooklyn felt good. I felt like a new woman inside, and I had never felt like that before. Business was business and we would forever be right-hand men, but I needed to give Que his space for now because I could tell this whole thing with Brook had him stressed.

Chapter 9 (Que)

I couldn't wait to get my hands on this bitch, Monique. Her trifling ass said she would never tell we fucked and the bitch did just that.

"I can't wait to put my foot off in this hoe ass," I thought to myself on my way to her house in full speed.

I lied and told her I wanted to come through and tear her off a piece of this dick. Of course, being the hoe she was, she agreed.

My situation with Cash had me fucked up. She was slipping away from me and fast, but fuck that, I couldn't let that shit happen. That nigga Nino was going to be laying next to fishes just like that nigga Carter. Yep, you heard right, *Carter.* The minute I felt Cash falling for him, I put some hot lead in his ass.

The Carlito Cartel had a price on his head for $100,000, so I linked up with them, knocked his dick in the dirt, sent them a few pics, and collected my cash. The Cartel was impressed. I had my bitch back, life couldn't have been better.

Cash was mine and even though we weren't official, she was still my bitch. She could fuck all these small time niggas but the moment I felt she was falling for them would be the end of their career. I know I sound like a hater and trust me, I'm far from that, but she had shit fucked up. I was the nigga she cried to when she was hurt, I was the one that held her down and bodied shit for her. I helped her in this game when her mother got knocked and not to mention, I'm the one eating the lining out her pussy.

Cash didn't know I knew, but I could tell she was falling for Carter. Her calls slowed down and the way she looked at him, alone, let me know she was falling for him, so I had to make a move fast. The day I killed Carter seemed like yesterday and it felt good to put him in his misery.

I called his phone and told him Cash had been shot. Even though he was mad at her about catching her with that other bitch ass nigga, I knew this plan would work. He came to my spot faster than a speeding lightning. He had his gun out, ready for war but little did he know, the war was with me.

"Is she ok?" Carter asked, rushing into the house.

"Man, I don't know, shit is not looking good."

"Where she at?"

"She's in the back room with the private doctor," I said as we headed to the back of the house.

I let him enter the room first, and when he turned around, I had my strap pointing right at his head. He tried to go for his gun but wasn't quick enough. I put six shots into his chest. I then cursed myself because my gun jammed. It didn't matter because looking at his lifeless body, I could tell he was dead.

I looked around the room while breathing heavy. I was impressed with my work. I was about to be a million dollars richer, and I'll be blowing Cash's back out in a couple days.

When I pulled up to Monique's house, all the lights were off except her bedroom light and the hallway light that led to the stairs. I knocked twice and waited for her to come down. Through the little glass windows, I could see her coming down the steps wearing only a silk red robe. I really wanted to fuck the bitch and then beat her ass, but her snitching ass disgusted me at just the sight of her.

As soon as she opened the door, *Wham!* I slapped the taste out her mouth. Her sexy smile was now turned into tears.

"What the fuck, Que?" she said in between tears.

"Bitch, you talk too much!" I slapped her again.

"What are you talking about?"

"Bitch, you know exactly what I'm talking about. I told you not to tell Cash we fucked!"

"I'm sorry, oh my God, I'm sorry," she cried while holding her jaw. I punched the bitch one more good time and then spit on her trifling ass. I shook my head at her and walked out the door just the way I had come.

117

I wanted to go to Keisha's, but I wasn't in the mood for her constant nagging, so I drove out to Cash's house.

When I pulled up, I punched in the security code at the gate and waited for it to open. I stuck my key in the front door and let myself in, and then I went to look for Cash. Just like I had figured, she wasn't there. I knew for a fact she was at that nigga Nino house. Just the thought of it was making my blood boil.

I went into her master bathroom and took a shower so I could get the little blood splatters off my arms. After I made sure to scrub Mo's blood off me, I stepped out, dried off, picked up my dirty clothes, and headed out the restroom. I dumped my white T-shirt in the wastebasket and pulled out an extra one from the pile of clothes I had kept over her house.

When I was finished, I went downstairs to make me something to eat because I was sure she wouldn't be home anytime soon. I pulled out a pack of chicken and a boxed mac and cheese. I stood over the stove like I was Chef-boy-r-Que.

After I ate, I went back to Cash's room and laid across her King size bed. I grabbed the universal remote and flicked through her cable channels until I was satisfied with an episode of Revenge. I loved this show because Emily Thorne was a cold bitch. Cash was the one that got me watching this shit. I actually laughed to myself because she had me watching all the female shit, even Love & Hip Hop.

I watched TV until I was tired. I wasn't going home, I would be here when Cash got home tomorrow and we had some major talking to do. This shit had to stop, and I was going to do anything in my power to make it.

I pulled out my Edge Plus and sent a text to Warden Scott so he could have Ms. Lopez call me ASAP. Warden Scott was cool as fuck and another crooked muthafucker on our payroll. He did anything we asked and we paid him well. We made at least a million just in one year off smuggling cell phones alone into the prison and that's not even the half of it. I knew I was wrong for what I was about to do but like I said, I was going to do anything in my power to fuck up what they thought they were about to have.

Brooklyn

When Cash and I pulled up to the house, I went straight into the shower. I needed to relax my mind so instead, I ran a bubble bath in my jacuzzi tub, hoping she would join me.

Shit was crazy already, and I had only been chilling with this girl for two days. I didn't want to put the blame on her but damn, I already had to body one of her ex-niggas for running up in my trap. I was on the verge of bodying her little boyfriend, Que if he kept getting beside himself. Not to mention, I was patiently waiting on that bitch Mo to cross me.

I had to give it to Lil Mama, though, the way she handled herself tonight had me damn near in love with her. I wasn't a lover boy type nigga, but I could really see myself with Cash. She was in full control of her own operation. She wasn't scared to pull a trigger and not to mention, she was the baddest bitch walking these Miami streets. Cash was beyond beautiful, smart, and if baby stayed around me like she been doing, I was gonna most definitely wife her ass up.

"What's on your mind?" Cash asked, walking in and taking a seat on the bed.

She broke my daze, so I continued taking off my clothes.

"Nothing, ma, I'm straight. What's up, you wanna take a bath with me?"

"Sure, I'd love that," she responded, taking off her pants and then her blouse.

I wanted to say fuck that bath and slam her sexy ass on the bed, but I held my composure and went towards the bathroom.

Lil Mama body was off the chain. I just prayed that everything would remain perfect because right now, it couldn't get any better.

I helped Cash into the tub and then climbed in behind her. She poured us a glass of Hennessy and we began our conversation, trying to get to know each other.

"Your hair looks nice, by the way."

"Thank you," she cooed, bashfully, and that shit was sexy as a muthafucka. It was crazy how she just bodied a nigga in front of me, then turned into a sexy, shy, school girl. This shit was driving me crazy.

"So, Cash, what's up, ma? A nigga curious about a few things."

"Uh oh," she laughed.

"Nah, ma, nothing like that. I'm just curious of why you don't have a man? I mean, I'm not stupid. I know you have male friends, but from the outside looking in, I'm sure it's nothing too serious."

"I don't know. Honestly, Brooklyn, I just don't have the time."

"Nah, it's more to it than that, so be real with a nigga."

She looked at me and sighed. I could tell she was gathering her thoughts, so I waited for her to open up.

"I've never been in love before. There was this one guy that I had fallen for, and I didn't realize I loved him till it was too late," she responded, and put her head down.

"So, what happened?"

"Well, to make a long story short, we had a falling out, and we didn't speak for weeks. Weeks later, I found out that he was killed," again, she put her head down.

"Damn, sorry to hear that."

"It's cool."

"So, what is it now? Is it because of him or is it because you're afraid of getting hurt?"

"Well, I can ensure you it's not about him," she smiled. "But I guess a part of me is afraid of getting hurt."

"Well, look, Lil Mama, I'm not gonna lie to you, I got a few female friends that I juggle but they ain't like you. I'm willing to fall back off them if you're willing to give me a chance with your heart."

It was like the words flowed smoothly off of my tongue. I couldn't believe I said it but every last word was true. I really liked this chick, and I was willing to fuck with her the long way. I knew it was going to be hard because I had Tiffany and that bitch could suck a mean dick, but for Cash, I would drop her ass too.

"Awe, Brooklyn," she was blushing, almost turning red.

"For real, ma."

"No lie, I really like you, but it's only been a few days. Don't you think that's a little too soon?"

"Cash, I was in love with you the first day I saw you at Esco house. I was so mad at that nigga, getting my work was my only focus at that time. I asked Esco about you and he told me he wasn't gonna give you to me because he was too close to your mom."

"Yeah, him and my mom are pretty close," she laid her head on my chest.

I kissed her forehead.

We talked about everything under the sun. The more we conversed, the more I felt myself falling for her. I just prayed the feelings were mutual because she was a tough cookie to deal with.

Cash lifted up and climbed on top of me, straddling my lap. She pressed her titties on my chest and kissed me like she was feeling a nigga I was smiling from ear to ear. Lil Mama knew exactly what she was doing. She had my dick hard as a muthafucka, and if she didn't move soon, I was going to slide it up in her ass. I was trying to contain myself, but her body was so fire, I damn near couldn't help myself. Fuck that, I was going for it!

I slid all 12 inches into her ass in one swift move, causing her to jump. Her pussy was so tight like she hadn't been fucked in a minute or she hadn't been getting fucked right. She was pulling on my dreads and moaning so loud, I was more than sure my security heard her.

"Throw it back, Lil Mama, throw that shit back," I said in a seductive tone and she was doing just that.

I flipped her ass into doggy style position and no lie, I had to give it to her because her pussy adjusted to my dick, making it almost impossible to go in and out. She started throwing it back like she was trying to win a competition and that shit was about to make me drop my load in her.

"Come on, ma, it's hot in here," I told her.

We stepped out the tub.

We didn't even make it out the restroom, I bent her ass over the sink and started punishing her sweet, good pussy like she'd been a bad girl. I wanted Cash to forget about any and every nigga in her life, so I was performing like the champ I was. Every time she screamed "*daddy*, I grew more and more inside of her.

I looked down at my dick as it went in and out of her tight opening and it was covered in white cream, which let me know she was cumming back to back. I was hitting it raw, something I never did because I didn't trust sack chasing hoes. However, it was something different about Cash. I was determined to put a baby in her, fast. I remembered her telling me she didn't want kids right now, but I didn't give a fuck. She was going to be my wife and we were going to have plenty Nino Jr.'s running around this muthafucka.

Chapter 10 (Cash)

The next morning, I was laying in Brook's bed with my pussy still sore from the beating he gave me. I had to admit, in all my years of fucking, I've never been fucked like that. Don't get me wrong, Que had the best dick a woman could ever imagine, up until now. Brooklyn's dick had to be over eleven inches and he knew how to work that muthafucka. It seemed as if this man didn't have any flaws and it was scary.

I laid in his arms as he rubbed his hands through my hair. All I could think of was the conversation we had last night before we started fucking. I didn't know what to say about becoming his girl, but I was willing. I didn't want to be in a relationship but this man was making me have a change of heart. I was actually flattered that he asked, so of course, I was going to take the chance. One thing I wouldn't do is let my guard down, but I was for sure going to make him a happy husband one day.

"So, what's up with you and this nigga Que?" he asked, and that shit, once again, caught me off guard.

"Nothing, Brook, I keep telling you that."

"Well, I just want to know because I can tell he's in love with you and I don't want that shit to get in the way. You belong to me now, so whatever it is, dead that shit ASAP, Cash."

"I told you, I've never fucked with Que."

"Yeah, a'ight, ma," he said and got up to head to the bathroom.

I walked up behind him, wrapping my arms around his waist. He turned to face me and kissed me. I went over to the second sink bowl and began my morning hygiene. The entire time I brushed my teeth, I could feel him watching me.

"So, what are you doing today?" he asked, drying off his face.

"Checking some traps. You?"

"Same shit, checking traps."

"Ok," I said and laughed because this is what our lives consisted of.

"I'm going to take you home. Pack you a bag for a few nights and make sure you grab something sexy so I can take you out tonight."

"Ok..." I agreed because it was pointless trying disagree.

Brooklyn stood his ground with me and I loved that shit. I was so used to niggas being submissive because of who I was. Everything I asked for or wanted was always yes. I got away with too much and it bothered me because I needed a man to put his foot down on me. The only nigga that stood his ground was Que, and little did he know, I craved the attention from him.

After a few more rounds of great sex, breakfast, and a swim, Brooklyn finally dropped me off.

When I walked through my door, something seemed strange. The smell of chicken filled the air and it was weird because my Chef only came when I called him. I ignored it and went to my room so I could soak my sore pussy and get my bag packed. I stayed so long at Brook's, I only had a couple hours to go check the traps and be ready for dinner.

When I got to my room, my bed wasn't how I left it so I scanned the entire room looking for clues. Whoever was there had taken a shower. That's when I looked at the TV, the channel on my television were all the clues I needed. I sat on my bed and that's when I zoomed into Que's shoes by the closet doors. All I could do was shake my head because this nigga was getting weirder and weirder.

Ring, ring, ring...

"Yeah?" he answered on the third ring.

"Nigga, was you in my house?"

"Why? Shit, you weren't there."

"I didn't ask you that, Que."

"Oh, it's a problem now?" He said in an aggressive tone. I just shook my head before answering.

"No, it's not."

"A'ight then," he hung up on me.

I looked at the phone in disbelief because this nigga was beside himself and it was starting to annoy me. I didn't even bother to call back because I didn't have time for Que's bullshit so I went and took my shower, and then looked thru my closet for something to wear.

After about thirty minutes, I settled on a sexy Primavera Couture nude dress that hugged my body perfectly. My nude Marc Jacob peep-toe pumps and matching bag. I adorned my wrist with a 25 karat princess cut bracelet and ring that sparkled like a glass chandelier. My hair was still on point, to my surprise, after what Brook served me with last night. I brushed it down, letting it flow over my shoulders. I applied my eyeliner, mascara, and gloss. Everything by MAC. I looked in the full-length mirrors and did a few spins. I was satisfied with my appearance and had to admit, I looked good as hell.

My phone rung and it was Nina. I quickly answered on the first ring. I had so much gossip to fill her in on and couldn't wait till she got off her flight from Jamaica.

"Hey, stranger."

"Hey, boo. Oh, my God, I miss you."

"I know, man, you been gone too long."

"I have, I'll be there tomorrow."

"Ok good, because I wanna hear about your trip. Also, bitch, I have so much juicy gossip."

"Oh, hell nah, I can't wait, spill it!"

We both laughed.

I went right in from Tiny and Mike to me and Brook, and not forgetting about Johnny's snake ass. We talked the entire ride to the trap. I promised to give her a call when I was done.

Nina was on a business trip. She was about to open a boutique in the A, Atlanta. I helped her with and I was so happy for her.

When I got to the trap, it looked empty, except for Blaze's car parked out front. I stuck my key in the door and it was silence throughout the entire house, so I merged to the back. I looked in the first room, it was empty. I then opened the second room and it was also empty.

"Damn, where the fuck everybody at?" I thought to myself as I opened the last room where Blaze always would be counting the money. what I saw before me when I walked in had my mouth literally on the ground.

"Oh, shit!" Blaze yelled, jumping up.

"What the fuck, I can't believe yall," I said, walking all the way in the room.

"Wait, let me explain," Tiny said, putting on her pants and trying to cover her titties with one hand.

"Have y'all lost yall fucking mind? Mike gone kill you muthafuckas!" I shouted at these two idiots.

Blaze had Tiny bent over the couch, ass in the air while hitting it like she belonged to him. I couldn't believe this shit, all I could do was shake my head. I closed the door and stormed out, but Tiny was hot on my heels, still putting on her clothes.

"Please don't tell, Cash, please," she said with pleading eyes.

"Look, this ain't my business but yall foul ass fuck, yo."

"I know, but I'm done with Mike," she said like that shit made a difference.

"So you fuck his homie?"

"It wasn't like that, I swear."
"Well, tell me what it was like, Tiny, because Blaze just had his dick in you and from what it seemed, you were enjoying every moment."

"I swear, it wasn't like that," she said again but I couldn't comprehend what the fuck she meant by *it wasn't like that*.

"Look, whatever yall got going on yall need to dead that shit, for real," I said to Tiny.

I then looked at Blaze as he came out the room. He rubbed his hands over his face and all he could do was shake his head. I did the same and stormed out the house. This shit had me hotter than fish grease and I needed to get out of there before I really went there.

Tiny was my girl, Blaze was my left hand, but so was Mike. We were a team and we didn't need shit getting in the way, especially over some pussy.

As I drove towards Brook's house, I figured I'd let it go for now. I wasn't going to let these two idiots fuck up my night, I was looking good and about to go on my first real date with my man so for now, I would brush it out my mind.

When I made it to Brooklyn's house, he was still upstairs dressing so I went to his bar and poured me a much-needed drink of Hennessy. I then went upstairs to join him. I plopped down on the bed and as much as I wanted to remain calm, I knew for a fact I looked stressed. Brook was in the bathroom so I used my time to gather myself. I sat pretty and waited for the door to open, and 15 minutes later…

"Damn!" he said when he stopped right in front of me. All I can do was smile at his etheusiasm.

"What, you like what you see?"

"Hell yeah, ma, you looking sexy as a muthafucka," he said while walking over to me.

"Move, bae, dang we ain't gonna ever leave," I giggled.

"Fuck all that," he said, lifting up my dress just enough for my monkey to creep out.

He went head first into my love box, circling my pearl tongue with the tip of his tongue. I laid back and wrapped his dreads around my fingers and pushed his head deeper into my pussy. He flickered at my clit and it was causing me to jump a little while I kept my hands in his dreads and twirling my hips to his rotation.

"Fuuuuck, Brook!" I shouted when I couldn't contain myself any longer.

Where the fuck did he learn how to eat pussy like this? I thought to myself while I continued to moan.

After about 30 minutes, I felt myself cumming and I wanted to be fucked. I was horny as hell and the minute I bussed, he lifted up.

"Go wash up, let's go," he smiled.

I was ready to jump up and sock his ass in the head.

I started to pout. "Come on, pa." I was craving the *D.*

"Nah, Lil Mama, we gonna save that for later," he walked towards the bathroom.

I looked at him as he walked out, still in shock.

"Fuck it," I thought to myself while walking to the bathroom to wash up. My knees buckled a bit but I felt great. That was officially the best head I ever had.

***

When we made it to the restaurant, I was impressed. It was a classy little hookah lounge. The theme was mimicking China. You had to sit on nice fluffy pillows and order through a tablet. The lounge was called Mahealani and that alone made me instantly fall in love.

"Hi, Mr. Carter? Same spot, as usual?" the front desk worker asked. She was a young Caucasian girl with blonde hair and a cute face. Her silk Chinese dress hugged her small frame, and I loved her bubbly attitude.

"Yes, Angelica," he smiled back at her.

We walked to the back, by a window, and it seemed secluded and away from the rest of the restaurant. However, I didn't complain, it was nice and quiet.

"So, Mr. Carter, huh? I asked. I was smiling, but inside I was really laughing because Brooklyn and Carter already reminded me a lot of each other and it just so happened his last name was Carter.

"Yeah, which will be your name soon, Ms. Lopez."

We both smiled.

"Hmmm, Cash Carter. sounds good to me," he gazed at me.

"So, you come here a lot, I see" I picked up the tablet so I could browse through the menu.

"I guess you can say that," he replied with his eyebrow raised. He picked up the tablet that was in front of him.

As he browsed the menu, a Caucasian guy in an expensive suit walked up with a nice looking older lady and asked if they could take a picture with him. Now this was really weird. The situation had me wondering if I was dating some sort of celebrity.

"Mr. Carter, would you do me the pleasure of taking a photo with me and my wife?"

"I would love to, sir," Brook stood up.

I sat back in my seat and smiled.

"Thank you so much, Mr. Carter. I love what you've done with the place," the guy said to Brook as he looked around the restaurant. That let me know why he was getting the special treatment.

The minute he sat down, he picked up the menu. He must have felt me grilling his ass because he looked up from the menu and smiled.

"What, ma?"

"Nigga, you know what. So, you're the owner, huh?"

He smiled again before responding. "Yes, Cash."

"So, why you didn't tell me you were the owner?"

"Same reason you didn't tell me you were the owner of Juice," he said with a smirk on his face. He sipped his glass of water.

"Mr. Carter, are you guys ready to order?" a waiter asked, smiling. The bitch was smiling a little too hard, on tops.

"You know what you want, ma?"

"Umm yes, I'll have the Fourchu Lobster, some Coconut Curried Shrimp and Rice with a glass of Williams Selyem Pinot Noir," I said and then looked up at the waitress.

"And you, sir?"

"I'll have the West Australian Lobster tails, the Chilean Sea Bass, and asparagus with a coke," Brooklyn ordered.

I smiled. I was so impressed with him. He was young, getting money, and who would ever think that a man with his thug persona would have such a successful business. Everything about Brooklyn screamed thug, from his tattoos to his walk, but he conducted himself very professional and I loved it.

"Why are you smiling so hard, Lil Mama?"

"I don't know… You, I guess."

"What about me?"

"Just admiring your thug personality with such class."

"Kind of like yourself?" he smiled, I blushed back.

Right when I looked towards the entrance, Que was walking in and guess who was on his arm? The bitch, Arcelie. Brook must have sensed something because he looked in the same direction I was looking.

"Ain't that your boy?" he said with an amused look on his face. He was trying read me but I wasn't going to break.

"Yeah, that's him and his girlfriend, Celie," I said. I was lying through my pearly whites with a fake smile, but he looked like he wasn't buying it.

When Que looked up, I shot him a look of death and that muthafucka smirked. He knew exactly what he was doing, by the look on his face, and from what it seemed, he didn't care about poor Celie because he knew I was going to chew her another asshole. She knew it too because she looked scared to death and kept her head down the entire time.

"You not gonna go over and say hi?" Brook said and he smirked.

"Nah, he still salty over Johnny."

"Oh ok," he said, then changed the subject. I was glad because I didn't feel like getting caught up in my lies. I knew I shouldn't have been mad but my blood was boiling. These two muthafuckas had something going all along and this shit had me hot.

Chapter 11 (*Que*)

Cash hadn't made any noise in the last couple months, ever since she saw me and Celie at that bitch ass nigga Brooklyn's restaurant. Either she was plotting or this bitch ass nigga had her nose so wide open, she didn't give a fuck anymore.

I ain't gone lie, I was iffy about showing up there but I had to get a good laugh. The expression on Cash's face was priceless. Thanks to my GPS I had on Cash's phone, I knew they were there. I was at Celie's house, beating her guts up when my phone alerted me when Cash was out of her boundaries. I made the nasty hoe get up without even washing her pussy. She slid her clothes on so we could make it there before they left.

From doing my homework, I knew Nino owned it and that was another thing on my agenda... to burn that muthafucka down. I was actually laughing to myself when my phone rang disrupting my thoughts.

"Hello?"

"Hey, Que."

"Hey, Ms. Lopez, how's it going?"

"Ok, so far so good. Check it, I'll be home sooner than you think, but don't tell Cash, ok?"

"Ok, I won't. That's kinda what I wanna holla at you about."

"Is everything ok, Que?"

"Not really, Ms. Lopez. Cash has been fucking with one of our enemies and she's been slipping on work. She's not collecting books anymore. Shit, she barely running her club or shop."

"Wow, so who's this nigga?"

"His name is Nino. He has a shit load of territories and I've heard he was tryna take over ours, so I think he's using Cash to get to us."

"So, have you spoken with her about it?"

"Yes ma'am, I have but she ain't trying to hear shit I'm saying."

"Ok, don't worry about her, I'm going to handle it. You just keep the business going, as usual."

"Ok, I got you."

"Ok, one." We disconnected.

I knew what I was doing was fucked up but I needed her head back on earth and out the clouds. Cash was slipping, and I was mad as fuck about it. But for now, I was going to get this money and forget about it all. But I promise you, sooner or later, I'd be head of this empire.

"Mo, come here and suck on this dick, ma," I told Monique. Without a word, she did as she was told.

I was still mad at her for telling, but with the fire ass head she had, I couldn't resist.

Brooklyn

I was going to be a daddy and I couldn't wait. I knew she was pregnant because she had been eating like crazy and her little stomach was bulging. She was iffy about keeping it but fuck that, if she killed my baby, I was going to kill her ass. Cash was carrying my first seed.

All the other bitches I had gotten knocked up in the past, I told them it was either me or the baby, and them hoes wasn't risking losing me. I didn't want a baby by these sack chasing bitches. They thought if they got pregnant, I'd be happy but they thought wrong.

Watching Cash run back and forth to the bathroom had me smiling. I felt bad because my baby was sick, but it was confirmation she was indeed pregnant.

"Here, ma," I handed Cash a Ginger Ale.

"Thank you."

"Man, you don't look to good, Lil Mama."

"I feel horrible, I'ma just lay down for a minute."

"Ok, I'm bout to go check some traps and I'll be back soon to check on you," I got up from Cash's bed to hit the door.

For the last few days, we been crashing at Cash's house. As much as I tried to convince her to move in with me, she wouldn't do it. She had a fat ass crib so I couldn't say I blamed her. But fuck that, I was ready to make shawty my wife and if she thought my seed was going to be living apart from me she had another thing coming.

I kissed her on the forehead and headed out the door. I hated leaving her like this, but I needed to make sure shit was running smoothly.

It had been months and this bitch ass nigga Ricky was still hiding. I was sure he was going broke so I knew sooner or later, he would come out and play. I knew he wouldn't get far because I had a price on his head. I knew the price I had on his ass, people would sell their own mama out. As I cruised the interstate, I thought about how good it was going to feel to put him to his misery, but first, I was going to make his bitch ass suffer.

I damn near didn't hear my phone ringing through the Bluetooth because I was in such a deep thought.

"Yo."

"What's up, Nino?"

"Who is this?"

"Oh, you don't know my voice?"

"Man, I'm bout to hang up. Who the fuck is this?"

"Its Monique," she said in a sassy tone.

"Oh, hey Mo," my voice softened a little the minute she said her name. I felt bad because Monique was hella cool, but I shitted on her with her boss.

"So, why haven't I heard from you?"

"Come on, ma, you know what it is."

"What, that you just said fuck me and started fucking my friend?"

"Look, ma, I'm not about to go into all this with you. Cash is my wife now and matter of fact, I don't think she will appreciate me talking to you. So, bye."

"I don't know why, she playing your stupid ass, anyway," she said, slickly.

"Girl, get the fuck out of here with that shit."

"Yeah, ok. Be stupid if you want," she laughed, but I was starting to get annoyed.

"Man, what the fuck are you talking about?"

"Sorry to be the one to break the news to you, but that baby she's carrying is Que's. Everybody knows but you, and I didn't want you out here looking stupid."

The minute she said that I hung up the phone. The bitch knew what she was doing and it worked. I jumped off the first exit and jumped back on, heading back towards Cash's house. My heart was beating a mile a minute. I was mad as fuck and prayed I didn't have to put my hands on her.

Man, this shit had a nigga hurt, I ain't gone lie. I asked Cash was she fucking that nigga over and over and each time she said no. If it's one thing I hated, it was to be lied to. It was a sense of disloyalty and that shit wasn't cool.

My thoughts were interrupted by my phone ringing again. "Yo?"

"Aye, Nino, it's Blaze. Can you come to the safe house? We got a lead on ol boy."

"I'm on my way right now."

"Ok, I spoke to Cash she's on her way here now," he said, but little did Blaze know, Cash was the last person I wanted to see.

"Yeah, aight," I responded and then ended the call.

I hated the fact of having to hold my composure but I couldn't wild out in front of her crew, especially that nigga Que. I couldn't give him the benefit of thinking he was getting to me so for now, I was going to let that shit ride.

I turned up my Rick Ross & Drake "Schemin" and did a 100 MPH to the safe house. This was all I needed, I had some frustration in me I had to let out and Ricky was about to be my victim.

When I pulled up, it looked like a Birdman video shoot with all the whips that was parked out front. I spotted Cash's baby pink Bentley and instantly got mad. I wanted to strangle her ass, but I just couldn't bring myself to putting my hands on a woman. My father was a stand-up guy and not once have I ever saw him put his hands on my mother or any woman, so it wasn't a trait.

Truth be told, these last couple days I had been falling for Cash but right now, I was hating her worse than an enemy.

The minute I walked in, she was the first face I saw. As much as I wanted to hug her or maybe even kiss her, I couldn't pull myself to doing it so I walked right past her ass and straight to Blaze.

"Nino, what's good, fam?" Blaze said, giving me dap.

Of course, Que had his face scrolled up, and Cash was sitting there with a confused look as to why I didn't acknowledge her.

"What's good, Blaze?"

"Nino, this is Marcus. Marcus, this is Nino. He's the brains behind the technology," Blaze introduced us and we both nodded our heads to each other.

"He has an address on Ricky bitch ass. It's his foster mother's house. We ran his info and turns out, the nigga real name is Alvin Sanders, his pops is Big Alvin Sanders," Blaze said, handing me a paper with an address scribbled on it.

"Wait, the notorious Big Al?" I asked. I couldn't believe this shit. "Big Al had something to do with my parents being killed," I said. I getting more upset than I already was. I just shook my head because this shit was a bit too much.

"Yes, the Notorious Big Al. You know this nigga personally, Nino?" Blaze said, shaking his head as well.

"Yeah, very personal. I'm the one who killed his bitch ass, that nigga had something to do with my parents being murdered and I'm more than sure he had something to do with my brother's hit too."

"Wow" was all Blaze said while everyone listened.

For some reason, this nigga Que had a stern look on his face when I mentioned my brother.

"If you guys would please do me the honor of letting me kill his bitch ass?"

Everybody nodded their heads, except Que. He was the only one with a smirk on his face and that shit was starting to annoy me. "Marcus, can you give me every address you have on Lil Al and anybody you can find associated with him?"

Marcus nodded his head, went into his computer and began his mission.

"Look, I have something to say," Que stood up like he ran the town. He put both hands on the table, leaning slightly forward, and began. "I think for the next few months we should handle all business without Cash."

Everybody looked at Cash.

She quickly jumped from her seat.

"What the fuck you mean without me, Que? I call the shots and if I say it's a go, then it's a go."

Que looked at her with a stern look on his face. "With all due respect, I don't think you should be in the field while you're carrying my seed, ma."

Everybody that was in the room mouths dropped.

My face tightened, I knew this nigga was trying to get under my skin, but he wasn't about to break me that easily.

"Oh, so it's his baby, Cash?" I looked at Cash and patiently waited for her to answer.

She put her head down, I could see tears fall onto her lap. I felt so bad for her, but it was time we got to the bottom of this shit.
h

"Yeah, Cash... tell this nigga who's baby it is," Que smiled. He was getting a kick out of all this and I didn't see shit funny.

Cash stood up, walked up on Que, and slapped the shit out of him. Cash then stormed out.

Que had the audacity to just laugh.

I got up to follow behind her because she had some explaining to do.

When I made it outside, she was nowhere in sight. When I walked back in, Blaze had a worried looked on his face. As bad as I wanted to kill this nigga Que right here where he stood, I had too much respect for Cash and her crew, so I let the nigga breath. It wasn't Que's fault, it was Cash that had been playing the both of us.

However, I hated was how this nigga was playing it. Que already knew my reputation in the streets just like I knew his. He wasn't no bitch nigga and I was far from it. So before we bodied each other, I was just going to fall back off Cash and let them do them.

Chapter 12 (*Cash*)

I was trying to get far away from Brook and Que fast as I could. I couldn't believe what Que had done. That muthafucka knew damn well we hadn't been fucking. I was only two months pregnant. I hadn't been fucking with Brook three months, and I hadn't fucked Que since I had been fucking with Brooklyn. The only reason I lied to Brooklyn was because I didn't want him to not trust me whenever I was around Que. But silly me, I knew sooner or later he would find out.

It was so much running through my mind, I needed a drink. At that point, I didn't give a fuck about being pregnant because truth be told, I wanted to get an abortion anyway. After seeing the look on Brook's face, that let me know we were through, and that shit was breaking me apart. Just that fast my whole world turned upside down in a matter of months and as of now, it was going for the worst instead of the better.

Then there was this shit with Ricky I had to stress about. This entire time he had been playing me, his whole identity was a fraud. I'm just glad I never fell in love with him. Everything about him had always seemed weird and now I understood why. He was plotting the entire time. I couldn't wait to get my hands on him

147

before Brook because I was for sure was going to murder his ass myself.

Dear Mama chimed from my purse distracting my thoughts. It was the private phone my mom had always called from. As bad as I didn't want to answer, I had to because I didn't talk to her much.

"Hey, mommy," I said, trying to sound cheerful so she couldn't tell that I had been crying.

"So, do I need to pass the throne to Que until you get yourself together?" She sounded upset.

"Huh?" I curiously to what she was talking about.

"You heard me, Cash! Do you need some time to get yourself together because if so, I can let Que take over the empire for now."

"Mom, what are you talking about?"

"I hear, whoever this nigga is, got you head over heels and knocking you off focus."

The minute she said that, it let me know she had talked to the infamous Que.

"Look, I'm fine. The business is running smoothly. My personal life has nothing to do with my business. You left me this empire and I'm going to finish running it like I have been doing. I'll kill Que or whoever else before they sit on my throne." I hated to get snappy with my mother but right now, she had me all the way fucked up.

"Well, you and this little boyfriend of yours need to dead that shit. I don't need you slipping over some nigga, Cash," she said, and it sounded like she meant business.

My other line beeped and it was Nina. Honestly, I didn't have anything else to say to my mother.

"Look, mom, I gotta go. Pedro is calling," I hung up on her.

I knew my mother like a book and she wasn't calling back, so I would deal with her when the time came around again. I had too much on my plate to be hearing her nonsense. What had me upset the most was she didn't even have her facts straight before she was already trying to knock my position. I wasn't worried about whatever hater lied on me nor her. This was now my empire and I'd die keeping it that way.

"Bitch, please tell me you back," I said to Nina, answering the phone. It wasn't Pedro. I lied to my mother to get her off the phone.

"Yes, where are you?"

"Oh my God, girl, going through it. Can you meet me at Juice?"

"How long?"

"I'm on my way there now."

"Ok, I'll meet you there."

"Ok."

Every few seconds, I looked in my rearview. It seemed as if this black Benz was following me. At first, I thought I was tripping so I turned down a side street and the car did the same. I pulled Dolly out the stash and sat her on my lap just in case I had to use her. I made another slight turn and still the car was behind me so I sped up.

The car sped up with me but couldn't catch me. I thanked God I had driven my Bentley. I was caught at a red light but easing through it. I grabbed my phone to call Blaze and the minute I looked up…

Boc! Boc! Boc! Boc! Boc! Boc!

My side window was shot out. I cocked Dolly back and let off eight rounds into the vehicle and pressed my pedal to the metal trying to get away.

Shit! I cursed myself because my phone slid under the gas pedal. It was hard for me to try and reach it and steer my vehicle at the same time. After struggling for a few seconds, I finally reached it…

Ratta tatt tatt...Pow! Pow! Pow! Pow! Pow! Pow!

I could feel my tire blow, then I lost control of the wheel and went flying into a brick building ahead. The impact was so hard, it made my body jerk forcefully and the airbags came out. I felt a stinging sensation that caused me to growl in pain. When I looked down, blood covered my entire top. I was hit in my chest and arm and that shit burned like hell. I was too weak to search for my phone. Next thing I knew, everything went black.

Nina

I pulled up to the club and didn't see Cash's car out front, in her usual parking spot, so I decided to go up and wait for her. Tonight was supposed to be a celebration, but how could I celebrate when my friend sounded like something was heavily on her mind. I had been in Atlanta meeting with some investors to close out the deal on my new boutique. I was a businesswoman in the making and
I was extremely excited. Cash had promised me she would help me get my boutique started and just like she promised, she delivered.

I owed Cash my life because, from the day I met her, my entire life had changed.

I was raped by my uncle Bruce as a child and when I told my mother about it, of course, she didn't believe me. Come to find out, her and uncle Bruce had a secret affair behind my aunt Michelle's back. Yes, her own sister's husband. Bruce was my step-uncle, but because he was around since I was a child, I looked up to him as blood. Up until the day he came into the bathroom while I was in the tub and forced himself on me. Nobody believed me but my big brother Day-Day. I knew my brother was crazy and that's why I didn't want to tell him and guess what, the same night I told him, he killed him. I felt horrible because now he was doing a bid upstate on not only the murder for Bruce but also a robbery they had been watching him on. I felt as if it was all my fault my brother was in jail and till this day, it haunted me.

I was working on my second bottle and Cash still hadn't shown up. I looked down at my phone to check the time and two hours had passed since I talked to her, so I dialed her number. It rang four times and went to voicemail so I called back. The second time I called, a very unusual male voice answered. I could tell the guy was white, so the first thing came to my mind was Cash got knocked by the police. I instantly hung up. I started panicking, not knowing what to do, so I dialed Que's number. However, before I could push send, Cash's number was calling back. I answered nervously, curious to why would the police be answering her phone.

"Hello?"

"Hi, ma'am, I'm officer Garcia from Miami Police Department. I'm having problems locating any family members for Cash Lopez. She was shot and is in surgery. Is it possible that you can get a hold of any of her family?"

I was so in shock, I couldn't even respond fast enough.

"Ye ye...yes, sir, I'm her sister," I told him then gave him my name. "What hospital is she at, sir? I'm on my way," I said in a panic, rising from the stool I was sitting on.

After he gave me all the info I needed, I was out the door.

On my way to the car, I called Blaze because if I had called Que, he would only make matters worse.

"Sup, Nina baby?" Blaze answered on the first ring.

"Blaze, oh my God, meet me at Miami Memorial, Cash was shot!"

"What the fuck?" Blaze shouted.

"Yes, an officer called me from her phone. All he said was she's in surgery."

"Aight. I'm going to hit Nino and Que, then I'm on my way."

"Oh shit, both her men," I said and we both laughed.

Man, we needed that laugh because right now, we were in a frantic and all we can do was pray.

When I made to the hospital, I went through the emergency doors and straight to the information desk.

"Yes, I'm here for a gunshot patient. Her name is Cash Lopez."

"And, you are?"

"Her sister. I. spoke with officer Garcia."

"Ok yes, she's on the 7th floor. Just wait in the lobby when you go up because she's still in surgery. Here's your pass, the elevator is to your left."

I took the pass, stuck it on my shirt, and headed to the elevator.

When I made it to the 7th floor, I took a seat and waited for the guys to come. I was so stressed I couldn't control my tears.

I prayed my best friend would be ok because if she wasn't it, would be hell in these streets. Ms. Lopez was going to kill any and everything she could get her hands on, not to mention the Cash Boyz, Nino, and Que.

I had to laugh because Cash had these niggas going. She always had that whip of appeal about her and now, she had the two cutest most powerful men ready to kill each other. The more I thought of her, the harder I cried. I couldn't control it, she was really all I had and I needed her here with me. I dropped to my knees and prayed to God she would pull thru this.

Blaze

I was more than sure this bitch ass nigga Ricky, Al or whatever his name was, had something to do with this. What I didn't understand was what the fuck happened. Cash was a trooper,

she was a gunner, a rider, and a real life trap girl. This was Ms.
Cash muthafucking Lopez, she never got caught slipping!

I had to be the bad news bearer for her little boyfriends.
Que didn't answer and Nino sounded like he was going to cry.

I had a talk with Nino after everybody left. I assured him of
the games Que was playing, letting him know Cash was not
fucking with Que like that. Que my boy, but I wouldn't be here
without Cash. I loved that girl like a sister and I'd do any and
everything for her. I've known many of Cash's little boy toys but
she was never open for anyone like Nino. Nino was a good dude
and in my eyes, he was perfect for her. Therefore, after all the
bullshit, I was going to holler at that nigga Que.

This shit was crazy, some heartache that I didn't need. I was
already going through enough bullshit with Tiny's ass. She had
been blowing up my phone but I made a pact to myself that I
wouldn't cross that line again. After Cash had caught us, I felt bad
as fuck. I knew I was wrong, man. Mike was my boy but damn,
Tiny caught me at a vulnerable moment. I was drunk and that was
the excuse I was running with. I prayed I wouldn't have to body
my boy over his wife but hey, I was the kind of nigga to shoot first
and ask questions never.

When I walked thru the hospital doors, I was escorted to
the 7th floor where Cash was still in surgery. Que and Nina were
already here and I actually had to laugh because when I called

Que, he didn't answer, which let me know he still had that tracking device on Cash's phone.

"Que is a wild boy, I swear," I said to myself, shaking my head.

Everybody was silent and looked stressed the fuck out, so I took a seat next to Nina and sat patiently waiting for the doctor's update. Ten minutes later, I had to make everybody laugh because this silent shit was killing me.

"Que, what the fuck you doing here so soon, nigga? You still got that tracking device on Cash's phone?" I laughed and everybody joined in. Que even smiled.

"You know I do, and if she gets a new phone, I'm going to track that muthafucka too," he said, laughing and we all laughed with him because we all knew he was dead ass serious.

Looking at Que, I could tell he was beating himself up behind the whole situation because when Cash flew out the meeting, it was because of his frivolous acts. I just stared at him for a minute and I could tell he was losing it but trying to keep his composure. Shit couldn't get any crazier, Nino walked in and I knew for sure that shit could get ugly I just prayed everybody would stay focused on the reason we were all here. He walked right up to me and gave me a pound then jumped straight to it.

"How's she doing, Blaze?" he asked and the entire time, Que was grilling Nino.

"Man, we don't even know, she's still in surgery but should be out soon."

He just shook his head and did what we all did and that was take a seat and stress.

The doctor finally came in and told us she was in recovery and was doing great. In about 15 minutes we can go see her for 20 minutes because visiting hours were over.

When we walked in her room, she was connected to a million machines but by the way her chest was heaving up and down, I could tell she was breathing and doing fine. She had a gash on her forehead and a cut on the side of her face. Other than that, she looked pretty good to have been in a shootout and accident all in one.

Mike and Tiny walked in and shit got really awkward. I avoided Tiny's eye contact she was trying to give me as much as I could. *"This bitch doing this shit on purpose,"* I thought to myself, but not taking my eyes off Cash.

Chapter 13 (*Cash*)

When I opened my eyes, I felt like I was in a dream. I had what seemed like 100 pair of eyes on me, which made me feel kind of embarrassed. I tried to fake sleep because I didn't want to deal with these two dumb ass niggas right now, but thanks to Tiny loud ass, she saw my eyes open and shut.

"Oh my God, Cash, you're awake, thank God," Tiny said, running towards me.

"Ouch, hoe!" She was squeezing the life out of me.

"Dang, you tryna kill her," Nina said, smiling. She ran over to us. Que was sitting in the chair across from me while Brooklyn stood by the window. I could tell he had a lot on his mind.

"Glad to see you are ok, baby girl," Blaze smiled and then kissed me on the forehead.

I kept quiet and smiled, I was happy to see my team by my side. As mad as I was at these two assholes, I was still happy to see them and most important to be alive. It was like my life flashed before my eyes. I was sure I was dead and thanks to god, I'm here and able.

"Ms. Lopez, glad you've joined us," the doctor said as he walked through the door.

I just smiled at him and waited for whatever he had to say.

"Well, we removed the bullet lunged into your chest, it didn't hit any main arteries, thank God. The second bullet went into your arm and came out of your side. It didn't shatter anything and you're very lucky, honey, because one 1 inch left, it would have shattered a main artery, causing you to need amputation. I do have some bad news. The baby didn't survive, I do apologize. You were about 14 weeks and 3 days on the ultrasound we conducted." He signed some papers, then he left as fast as he came.

Que's punk ass was smirking like always, and Brook looked hurt. Fourteen weeks had let everybody know it was Que's because I had only been with Brooklyn about 12 weeks. I really didn't feel bad because I hadn't slept with Que since I'd been with Brook and nothing could make me feel any different.

Que had been by my side since day one. True, he was acting off emotions but he was my right hand and we shared something special. At this point, all I could do was hope that me and Brook could move past this and start new. True, I was wrong for lying, but that wasn't enough to hold against me.

I looked over at Mike and he looked lost into space. I had damn near forgotten about the whole incident with Blaze and Tiny thot ass. Everything seemed fine, which let me know Mike still didn't know. I prayed he would never find out.

Brooklyn walked by my bed side, which knocked me out my thoughts. He looked me in my eyes. We held each other's gaze for a long time before he grabbed my hand and spoke.

"I'm glad you straight, Lil Mama."

For the first time since I had woken up, I spoke. "Thanks," was all I said with a smile because I really didn't know what else to say.

I snuck peeks over at Que and of course, he looked like he was ready to punch the shit out of Brook. But he knew I wasn't having that shit.

A nurse walked into the room to let us know visiting hours were over, but on her way out Brooklyn, stopped her.

"Ma'am, is it ok if she has one visitor spend the night?"

Everybody looked at me. I was shocked he had asked.

"Sure, are you Ms. Lopez's significant other?"

Before Brook could answer, Que jumped up and protested.

"This nigga is not staying here," Que looked at me.

"Que, don't start yo shit!" I shouted. I'm sure he could see the veins popping out my neck, which let him know I wasn't playing. I looked at the nurse as she stood there with a shocked expression. "Yes, this is my fiancé, nurse, and yes, he could stay."

Que shook his head. It looked like he was ready to cry, but I knew Que too well and he was too gangsta for that. He got up and left without another word, followed by everyone else. Everyone hugged me, promising they'd be back tomorrow.

Here I was, shot the fuck up, laying in this hospital bed, damn near had my life taking from me and this nigga Que was still on his bullshit. I knew that Brook would be leaving tomorrow morning to at least change his clothes, so I was going to call Que back to the hospital because we needed to talk.

"How you are feeling, ma?" Brook asked, sitting at the foot of my bed.

"I'm fine, Brook. A little pain in my side but I'm ok, for the most part."

"That's good, man. You had a nigga scared to death."

"How did you find out?"

"Blaze called me."

"Oh, ok."

"So, what happened, ma?" he asked with his face tightened. The look he wore let me know all hell was about to break loose in these streets.

"It was crazy, I was on my way to meet Nina at Juice, and I noticed a black Benz tailing me. I made a few turns, which let me know it was for sure following me. I dropped my phone and when I went to retrieve it, they started busting, so I busted back."

"With Dolly, right?" he asked in concern.

Dolly was registered to me, so defending myself would be my alibi. The last body I had was Johnny, and I made sure to use Que's gun.

"Yes, with Dolly."

He sighed in relief. He got silent and I knew why. Therefore, I cut to the chase.

"Look, Brook. I'm sorry about everything with Que," I spoke sincerely. I needed this man to understand every word I said and that I meant it.

"So, it was his baby, huh?"

"Yes," I said just above a whisper.

He put his head down.

"I'm sorry for lying to you. I just didn't want you to feel uncomfortable around me and Que. I'm going to be honest with you, me and Que have been messing around for years. I never wanted a relationship with him because we were on the same team."

"Have you been fucking him since we been together?"

I looked him square in his eyes with every ounce of sincerity.

"No I haven't, Brooklyn, I swear."

He just nodded his head.

I grabbed his hand and to my surprise, he didn't object. "I love you, Big Poppa."

"I love you too, Lil Mama. But don't think you are off the hook. Anything you got going on with this nigga, DEAD IT! If it ain't about yall business, that shit is a wrap, ma. Because next time he tries and flex, shit gon get real ugly. I've been giving this nigga passes because I got love for your team, but this nigga better stop acting like he don't know who the fuck I am." Brooklyn sounded like he meant it.

Brooklyn got up and walked over to the window and looked out into the night's sky. It was 4:30 in the morning, so the sky was so clear. You could see every star that brightened the horizon. He wore his dreads pinned back and his almond shaped looked as if he had so much pain and hurt. From the conversation we just had, I knew I relieved him of one less burden. Therefore, the only thing left now was to get a hold of Ricky.

***

The next morning, Brooklyn left to go get dressed. He promised he'd be back, but I told him to take his time because I secretly needed to speak with Que.

The doctor came in before Brook left and informed us that I would be leaving in two days. I was so excited. I had shit to do, and Ricky bitch ass was my first priority.

Later on in the afternoon, after I ate lunch, the nurse thought it would be best if I walked the hospital. I was a bit nervous at first and my arm was killing me, but I had to get up out this bed. I was walking slow as hell, trying to hold my IV pole steady. My legs were trembling a bit but the more I walked, the faster my pace became.

I jumped on the elevator to wander around the hospital, exiting the 9th floor. When the doors opened, I knew I had to be at Labor and Delivery because of all the teddy bear and balloon patterns that gracefully decorated the walls. Everything seemed so peaceful and it helped put my mind at ease. The cries from the babies made me think of the what if's. What if I did have my baby? How would things be with me and Que as parents? No, I didn't want my baby, but just like any other woman, I wondered what it would have been like to mother a child.

Looking through the crystal clear glass window, I admired the many baby feet that stuck out from the glass bassinet. I looked over towards the nurse's station, and me and Que locked eyes. My eyes then fell onto the newborn baby he was cradling in his arms.

"Ugh, this bitch had her baby," I thought to myself while mugging Keisha.

He looked surprised to see me, I could see the frustration in his eyes. I gathered myself and tried to walk away as fast as possible, but I failed because the pain was shooting through my entire side. I limped my way back to the elevator, hopped on quickly and pressing the 7th floor.

Before the door could fully close, Que stuck his Nike inside to keep it from closing. I sighed because I was in pain and not in the mood to talk. Que was standing there looking like he had a million things on his mind and didn't know where to start so I took the lead. I stepped off the elevator and sucked it up like a big girl.

"Que, I didn't mean to catch you, but we need to talk."

He walked over and stood against the wall. The look he was wearing let me know that he knew what it was going to be all about.

"I'm listening," the nigga had the nerve to say, crossing his hands over his chest.

"Look, Quintin, we can't keep doing this. You have to live your life and I have to live mines. One minute, you are causing chaos in my life over a baby you knew I didn't want, and then next, you are in labor and fucking delivery with another bitch. I can be immature like you and drag that bitch by her hair, but what would that change? She's gonna always be your child's mother, she's forever a part of your life now."

He stood there silent, so I continued. "Please, stop tripping. I love you, but you already knew, us as a couple, wouldn't work. I'm with Brooklyn now and that's how it's gonna be."

He still remained silent, but his nose flared from the mention of Brook's name. He leaned off the wall and stood straight up.

"You got that!" he said, turning around to walk away.

This muthafucka left me standing there like I wasn't shit. But I didn't sweat, it I just prayed he would let this shit go and move on. I walked back to my room and laid down. I couldn't get Que off my mind, but like I said, it was time for us to cut the shit.

Chapter 14 (*Cash*)

Things were going smooth for the past couple months. My body healed great and the scar on my face healed perfectly, thanks to Aloe Vera.

Que and I had been conducting our business as usual, but he barely spoke to me. I was tripping because he was out of me and Brook's way.

Brook and I were doing great. I was in my room getting ready to go out on the town with him. We still hadn't caught up with Ricky, but we had heard about a surprise party his baby mama was throwing for him this weekend at club Rain. Therefore, we were patiently waiting for Friday to come because we were going to go in with guns blazing.

I slipped into my clothes and then headed out the door. I hit the alarm on my G-Wagon and slid into the driver seat. I put on my Nicki Minaj Pinkprint CD and buckled my seat belt.

When I pulled out the driveway, I noticed a dark blue Crown Vic on the corner. The tint was so dark, I could barely see inside. However, I could see a male figure inside. I didn't pay it any mind, I just went about my business to go meet Brooklyn.

Lately, Brook was pressing me hard about moving in with him, but I wasn't ready for that. Don't get me wrong, I loved Brook but I loved coming home to my own space, at times. I couldn't leave Pedro, and Brook insisted moving him into his back house but that was something to think about.

I drove to Brook's house in deep thought. The last six months were crazy.

When I pulled up, Brook was outside waiting for me.

"Hey, Lil Mama," he said as he walked to my car, looking good as fuck. My pussy instantly started jumping. I had to squeeze my legs tight because it felt like my juices would start flowing any minute.

"Hey, Big Poppa," I said, stepping out the car to give him a hug.

"Damn, ma, you must miss a nigga."

"Brook, we just left each other this morning," I laughed.

"Yeah, if you move in, we'll never have to leave each other."

"Oh my god. Bae, don't start," I said, getting in the passenger seat. He jumped in and we headed out.

"So, where we going?" I asked, buckling my seatbelt,

"We're going to my brother's wife house first. It's my niece's birthday, I'm going to give her some money. We're not staying, I'm going to just drop it off."

"Oh, ok," I replied, leaning my seat back.

About an hour later, we pulled up to a nice brick home in the West beach area. Brook pulled into the driveway and parked. He hopped out and told me he'd be right back.

When the front door opened, two kids ran up to him screaming uncle Brook. He hugged them in one big group hug then a woman appeared from the house, who I assumed was his brother's wife. He hugged her, said a few words, and then they walked back towards the car.

"Lydia, this is Cash, my lady. Cash, this is Lydia my brother Bronx's wife."

"Nice to meet you, Lydia," I extended my hand for a handshake.

She was a beautiful lady with a pretty cocoa complexion and jet black curly hair that she wore in a high bun. I was puzzled because I'd seen her somewhere before. I couldn't quite put my finger on it but I had seen her somewhere before. If it was one thing I never forgot and that was a face. I brushed it off and she began talking to me.

"It's so nice to meet you, Cash. I'm so happy my brother found somebody as beautiful as you."

"So, what you saying, my bitches be ugly?" Brook said, playfully punching her in the arm.

We all laughed.

"Nooo, bro, I'm just saying, Cash looks like she has sense and manners."

"Oh ok, because I was about to say."

"Thank you, Lydia," I smiled.

She then looked at Brook. "Brooklyn, are you coming by next Sunday for the party?"

"Yeah, you know I can't miss it to save my life, sis."

"Ok good and make sure you bring Cash with you"

"I sure will, if she's not busy."

"Shut up, bae," I said, now punching him in the arm.

"I'd love to come. How old is she turning? So I'd know exactly what gift to get her."

"She's turning 13 years old."

"Awe, a fresh teen. Yes, I'll most definitely be there," I said smiled.

After we talked to Lydia for a little while longer, I had Brook drive me to the Benz dealership. With all the things going on in my life, I almost forgot about Niy-Niy's graduation. I was going to surprise her with a ride. I knew Nikki would die, but hey this girl deserved it. It was a privilege to attend college and unfortunately, I didn't get the chance. Back in high school, I was a straight A student and had plans of becoming a lawyer. Diane and I were supposed to attend law school together but life had other plans for me. I graduated high school with honors then my mother got knocked, so instead of furthering my future, I was stuck running one of the biggest drug enterprises in the state of Miami.

When we pulled up to the dealership, we went in and were greeted by the receptionist. She was a brown skin girl who looked kind of ghetto to be working at a dealership, but hey, I guess she had the skills to be there.

"What's up, Nino?" she said, cheesing all in Brook's face.

I looked at him but he avoided eye contact with me. I reminded myself to check his ass in the car, but for now, I was there for one thing.

"Umm yeah, I'm trying to find a whip. Something nice, but not to flashy, for an 18-year-old," I said, making the bitch look at me.

"Oh ok, follow me and I'll show you a few cars," she said while walking from behind the desk.

On her way past us, she eyed Brook and it was one of those evil eyes, like she'd known him personally. Brook wasn't even bothered by the bitch, so I didn't sweat it. We walked out to the lot and a cute silver Benz caught my attention.

"Yes, this the one," I said, smiling and walking around the car.

"This car is 94,000," she said in a sassy tone.

"I didn't ask how much it was. Just start the paperwork," I snapped right back at the bitch. She had the nerve to roll her eyes.

"This bitch got one more time and I'm about to mop the floor with this hoe," I thought to myself walking away.

I opened the door and inspected the interior. I started the car and peeped the navigation and the wood grain on the dash. *"Yes, this the one,"* I said to myself. I looked over to tell Brook come check it out and I could see the bitch saying something to him, but snapping her neck at the same time.

"Umm, what's up Nino?" I said, walking up on his ass, sarcastically.

"This the one, ma," he tried to say like his ass wasn't up to no good.

I just shook my head and walked off.

After signing all the paperwork and paying the money for the car, I stormed off to the car, not saying a word to his stupid ass. I don't know why, but I was a bit jealous and this shit was not me. He kept trying to make small talk but I didn't have shit to say to his ass.

I was sending Nikki to pick up the car tomorrow, once the paperwork was complete. I thought about coming back to the dealership myself so I could slap the hoe that was all in my man face.

I buckled my seatbelt, sat back, and started pouting. I gazed out the window and every now and then, I could feel his eyes watching me.

We pulled up to the beach and I was mad because right now, I didn't want to be around his ass, but it was too late. I jumped out the car, he jumped out behind me and started calling my name. I ignored his ass and tried to walk off, only to be snatched the fuck up.

"What the fuck is your problem!" he said, yelling at the top of his lungs, and grabbing my arm.

"I ain't got no problem," I yelled back, trying to snatch my arm away, but he had a tight grip on me.

"Man, you tripping, ma!"

"Nigga, you got me fucked up!" I said, poking my finger into his chest.

"Cash, don't make me fuck you up out here in front of all these people."

"You ain't gon do shit! You disrespectful, muthafucka!"

"How? How the fuck am I'm disrespectful?"

"Who the fuck is she, Nino?"

"Man, that bitch ain't nobody."

"Nobody? Nigga, I can't tell that she ain't nobody, the way yall was smiling all in each other fucking face! Take me the fuck home, Nino!" I yelled, jumping back in the truck.

He stood there in silence for a minute and then hopped in the driver seat to pull off.

Brooklyn

The ride back to my crib was a silent one. Cash was quiet and honestly, I didn't know what to say to make her feel any better. Tiffany stupid ass knew exactly what she was doing at the dealership. As much as I tried to ignore the hoe, she was way out of line for that little stunt she was pulling. I didn't mean to disrespect Cash but the minute she got inside the Benz to check it out, that gave Tiffany the perfect opportunity to press me about not talking calling her or answering her calls. I'm not going to lie, I had got some head from the bitch while Cash was recovering from her gunshot wounds. A nigga had to let it out. Every time I tried to get some from Cash, she complained about her wounds. I was still caught up over her and that nigga Que, so when Tiffany hit me up, I didn't resist that fire ass head.

Cash was sitting in the passenger seat quiet and every now and then, I stole a glance. Her ass looked sexy as fuck over there pouting. As bad as I wanted to grab her hand, she was acting stubborn so I gave her space. My phone rung through the blue tooth and it was a number I didn't recognize. I wanted to ignore it so bad, but Cash shot me a look that read *answer it nigga*, so I did just that.

"Yo!"

"So, you just say fuck me and then disrespect me by bringing bitches to my job?"

The minute she spoke, I knew all hell was about to break loose. But to my surprise, Cash was still staring out the window and hadn't even looked my way.

"First of all, watch yo muthafucking mouth. Second, I didn't know you worked there, Tiff, and third, you're not my bitch so why the fuck are you worried about who I take anywhere?"

"Oh, so now you got a bitch," she said, sounding like she was on the verge of crying. "Well, what about me, Nino? You just up and leave me hanging. I thought we had something," she said, followed by sniffles.

"Look, ma, we didn't have shit and I told you that over and over. And yes, if you must know, yeah I got a fiancé, so lose my fucking number."

"What! So, it's like that, Nino?"

"Man, get the fuck off my phone, yo!"

"Nigga, you weren't saying that when that bitch was laying up shot the fuck up and you had yo dick all in my fucking mouth!" Click… The bitch hung up.

I didn't know what to say, but I needed to think fast because Cash was grilling me with the coldest look.

I pulled into my driveway and parked. I was waiting for Cash to get out the car so I could pin her ass up, but she jumped from my passenger seat to her driver seat and locked the doors before I could open it.

"Man, ma, let me just holla at you," I knocked on the window.

"Nah, go holla at the bitch that's been sucking yo dick, nigga. I'm out."

"That bitch lying, ma."

I was trying to plead my case but that shit fell on deaf ears because she was already in gear backing up. I had to jump back so she wouldn't run a nigga foot over trying to get out the driveway. I stood there stunned because I knew she was pissed.

"Damn, I fucked up," I thought to myself while shaking my head.

When I got in the house, I was hungry as hell. But the way I was feeling, I knew I wouldn't be able to eat. I probably lost the best thing that ever happened to me because of my selfishness. Cash was laid up with bullet wounds and instead of me being by her side, I was getting my rocks off by a real thot bitch.

I called T-Mobile to change my number because I wasn't about to get caught up with that punk bitch again. I shot Cash the new number and just like I figured, she didn't reply.

I headed up to my room and hopped in the shower. I couldn't get Cash off my mind, but I figured sooner or later, she'd come around.

I laid in my bed and flicked through the channels. I was trying to watch some TV so I could get my mind off her and before I knew it, I dozed off.

I jumped up out my sleep to the sound of my house phone ringing. I knew for sure it was Cash so I couldn't stop smiling.

"Just come over so we could talk," I said, answering the phone.

"I'll be over there in a minute, baby," Blaze said, laughing through the phone.

"Shut yo ass up, nigga."

"Sup, Nino?"

"Shit… man, just home, chilling."

"I been tryna hit Cash, man, she ain't answering."

"She's mad at me right now."

Blaze chuckled.

I told him what had happened and he promised me he would go over to check on her.

I laid back down.

As I laid in bed, I couldn't help it, I picked up my phone and scrolled through Cash's Facebook. I wasn't no social media type nigga, but Cash talked me into getting a Facebook and

Instagram so she could do all that girly shit and tag me in her post. At that moment, I was happy I did have it because I knew she wouldn't call me. But, at least, I could see her post. Her profile picture of me and her at the beach was removed and she now had a picture of herself holding Gutta. I scrolled to her first status and it read…

Niggas Lie, Bitches Lie, but Numbers Don't #MOE 13 minutes ago.

Her second status read…

Spilled milk... 40 minutes ago.

That status had a nigga feeling bad as a muthafucka, so I shot her an inbox… *Look ma I'm sorry about everything, can you come over so we can talk.*

After about 30 minutes, she hadn't responded and didn't even bother to open the message. Her inbox said she was active now so I knew she saw it. I just sat the phone down.

I felt like I had to get out the house, so I got up and slid into some Drugs sweats and a white T-shirt. I slid in my white Air Force Ones, grabbed my keys, and headed out to check some traps because just like Cash said MOE (money over everything).

***

The next morning I woke up, the first thing I did was check my phone. Cash hadn't called and the shit had me feeling some type of way. All night, I tossed and turned because I wasn't used to sleeping alone anymore.

I picked up the phone and dialed her number and like I figured, she didn't answer. Yesterday, she mentioned going to the shop to pick up her dough, so I was about to head up there to see if she had made it. I was about to get dougie, not that I wasn't all the time, but I was about to get on my GQ shit and get wifey back.

After taking a hot shower I slid into some faded blue Robin's Jeans, a white tight fitted T-shirt, and a navy blue blazer. My feet were laced in some white Balenciaga's. I threw on my Cuban link chain with the pendant that read "MOE" just to be funny and settled with my 18 karats blocked studs. I pulled my dreads break into a pony and left some hanging in the back how she liked and then sprayed her favorite Issey Miyake cologne.

On my way down, I bumped into my maid Blanca who was on her way to clean my guest rooms. Blanca knew my room was off limits and Cash was always the one who cleaned it.

"Hey, Blanca."

"Como Estas, Mijo?" she said, smiling at me as she entered the room.

"I'll be back later."

"Si, senor," she nodded her head up and down.

When I stepped outside, I was greeted by the nice hot sun that I actually had to squint my eyes from the beam that was blinding me. I called my driver Eddie so that he would drive me around town.

When he pulled up, I hopped in the back of my Maybach and hit the button on the sunroof, and just like that, the entire ceiling was missing. I grabbed the remote and pressed play on my six CD changer. The first song to come on was Meek Mill and Nicki Minaj "Bad for You." Damn, that made me think about Little Mama instantly. It was one in the afternoon so I knew by now she would be there.

Thirty-five minutes later, we pulled up and I hopped out, making sure I didn't scuff my kicks on the curb. I walked through the door and it seemed like the whole room had stopped. The bitch Mo was shooting me daggers like she did every time I walked in, and truthfully, the hoe betta had been lucky she still had a job. If I had told Cash she was the one that told me she was pregnant by Que, she would have been got her ass whooped and fired. I didn't pay that bitch any mind, I just walked to Cash's office, hoping she'd be inside.

When I opened the door, the room was empty. Therefore, I went to holla at Nikki and see if she knew where Cash was at.

"Hey, Nikki," I said, giving her a hug. "Where's my wife at?"

"What you do now, nigga?"

I just laughed. "Why I had to have done something?"

"Because, nigga, you asking me where yo wife at. If anybody know where she's at, it's you, Nino."

All I could do was shake my head. "Naw, ma, it ain't nothing like that."

She gave me a suspicious look like she did not believe a word I was saying.

"She called about an hour ago saying she was on her way."

"Oh, ok. Well, are you busy?"

"I have a client coming about 3:30. Why what's up?"

"I need my shit re-twisted."

"Oh hell no, Nino. Yo ass got too much damn hair."

"Awe, Nik, come on, ma. Don't be like that, you know my tips be good."

She just looked at me and shook her head. "Come on, nigga. I ain't got all day," she said while holding up the cape for me to put on and take a seat.

Right before we could start, Nikki's phone rang. I wasn't trying to be all in shorty business but I couldn't help but hear her conversation.

"You going to Juice tonight?" she asked whoever she was talking to.

I couldn't hear what the caller was saying, but Nikki just kept saying yeah, yeah, and then she stated Quan's birthday party was going up tonight. I acted like I wasn't paying attention, but I was all ears.

Quan hadn't hit me lately. I was sure if it was because he knew I was dating Cash. I couldn't believe it because Quan wasn't the type of nigga to be on no hater shit. But I didn't give a fuck, I was up in there tonight and he wanted to flex, then it was kill or be killed.

After about an hour and a half, we were done with my hair and Cash still hadn't shown up. Therefore, I left the shop and headed to get something to eat.

I dialed her number and she still wasn't picking up, so I went to her Facebook. Her last post was the one from last night, so I went to her Instagram and she had posted a plate of food about 39 mins ago. I could see a second plate by her plate but not the person she was with. I instantly got heated.

Damn, it ain't even been 24 hours and already she had moved on. I couldn't even be mad, though. Nah, fuck that, I was mad. I accepted the shit with her and Que, and I even forgave her for the whole baby thing. Now here she was, tripping over some shit she didn't know was true or not. What was fucked up was she wasn't even giving me a chance to explain, she just turned her back on me and that shit had me stressed.

"Man, fuck her," I thought to myself and I meant it. I wasn't about to keep calling her and stalking her shit like some sucka ass nigga so I went on about my day.

Chapter 15 *(Cash)*

As bad as I didn't want to go out, I had to be at the club
tonight to make sure Quan's party went well. This party was talked
about and what was really crazy, he could bring the city out on a
Thursday. I had all the dancers ready for tonight and even a few of
my barbers were coming to work, along with Nikki. Nina and I
were out to breakfast and afterward, we were going to hit up the
mall for something to wear tonight.

"Girl, what's up with you and your bae?"

"Ugh, change the subject, bitch."

"No Cash, I want to know. I like Brooklyn, so I hope you
let that shit go."

I sighed. Everybody was team Brooklyn and that shit was
driving me bananas. Even Blaze took a liking to him and Blaze
didn't like anybody.

"So, we went to the Benz dealership to get a Niy-Niy's car
and some thirsty hoe was grinning all up in his face."

"What? So, who was the bitch?" Nina asked with a stunned
look on her face.

"Girl, some bitch named Tiffany. Peep game," I said
waving my hand for her undivided attention. "So, on the way

home, the bitch called, talking bout she just sucked his dick a couple months ago while I was shot up."

"What? You are lying! I mean I'm sure the bitch heard you got shot, Cash. The streets be talking."

"True, but fuck that... that nigga was laid up, pillow talking with that bitch. Fuck him, Nina! Anyway, how the boutique coming along?" I asked, changing the subject.

"It's so bomb! When we gone have the grand opening?"

"Whenever you want to have it, you know I'll help out, ma."

"I'm so excited. As a matter of fact, I have a piece for you in the trunk."

"I'm happy for you, ma, you deserve it."

After we were done eating, we went off about our day.

Club Juice (Cash)

It was right after midnight when we walked in Juice. I had a full staff so I didn't have to work as hard. Honestly, I told everybody that I was there to work, but I was there to get my party on. I strutted through my club like the million-dollar bitch I was. I was feeling myself, and I didn't give a fuck about nothing.

It was some fine ass niggas in attendance and the way to get over one nigga was to move to the next nigga and I planned on doing just that.

When I stepped in my VIP section, I was greeted by Mike and a bottle of Belaire. I took the wine glass and filled it up, taking a seat to wait for Nina to come back from the restroom.

"Mike, what's up, pa?"

He sat down right next to me and he had this look on his face that I couldn't quite put my finger on.

"Shit, I need to holla at you, Cash," he leaned over towards me.

"I'm all ears."

"I need to cop 32 bricks."

"Mike, not here."

"I just need to know if you have them?"

I just shook my head because this nigga knew I don't conduct drug deals in my place of business. Him asking me about drugs in my club didn't sit too well with me.

"Mike, we will holla about that tomorrow, ok?"

"Ok," he replied, but he started scanning the room like he was looking for somebody.

"What's up with you, where you been?"

"Huh? Oh, shit, I been around. I just been dealing with this shit with Tiny."

"Oh ok… yeah, I haven't talk to her in a while."

"Yeah, she straight," he said, picking up his glass and gulping it down in one swallow.

Nina came back and took a seat next to me. She then poured herself a glass. After I refilled mines, we walked to the edge to look down at the dance floor. It was popping down there and as soon as our drinks kicked in, we were about to go turn up. We were looking bomb, as usual. I bent down to make sure Dolly was tucked tight in my boot.

An entourage of niggas walked in and Quan sexy ass was leading the pack. I knew he was still salty about Brooklyn, so I ignored his ass. He walked to his section and before he sat down, he looked in my direction and we looked eyes. I quickly turned my back to him and began talking to Nina.

"Ugh, bitch, let's go downstairs," Nina said, moving from side to side like she was ready to shake her tail feather.

As soon as Work by Rihanna came on, we started dancing. We knew we weren't going to make it to the dance floor in time, so we danced right where we were standing. We were imitating the video and doing Ri-Ri's dance she did in the video. My white leather skirt swayed with every beat my hips went, I was getting it.

When I looked over at Nina, she was in a zone like she was in the video in her mind. Poppy came out of nowhere and started grinding on me. When I looked up, Quan's eyes were on us heavy.

I don't know why I felt uneasy, but I stepped back a little, and when he nodded his head, I smirked at him. He picked up his bottle but didn't take his eyes off us. Nina jumped behind him so we had him in a sandwich and he bent down to whisper in my ear.

"What's up, ma? Where you been?"

"I've been busy," I said in an annoyed tone. I hadn't answered this nigga calls in months, which should have told him I was dodging his ass.

"Is that right? Are you coming home with me tonight?"

"Umm, I can't... I have to stay behind and help clean up."

"Oh, ok," he replied.

Before he could say anything else, I told him I'd be back, I had to pee. I grabbed Nina's hand and pulled her towards the restroom. When we got by the restrooms, we both started laughing.

After using the restroom in my office, we began watching the entire club on my high tech cameras. I had 13 monitors installed on the wall that centered in on every entrance, exit, corner, and the stairwells. There were four cameras in the VIP section so we took it upon ourselves to spy on Quan and his boys.

"Wait, bitch, is that Brooklyn?" Nina said, grabbing my undivided attention.

"Bitch, where?" I yelled, running to the camera she was looking at.

"Damn, they deep as fuck, and who's the little bitch all in his face, Cash?"

"Bitch, that's Marie hoe ass," I said. I was getting heated. She was whispering something into his ear and what was pissing me off was the fact that he didn't tell the bitch to back the fuck up. Instead, he stood there smiling like the shit was funny, but I had something funny for his ass.

When Nina and I walked back into the VIP section, I was happy his section was two booths down, even though we were outside of all the booths where we could be seen. It was me and Nina's booth, Quan's in the middle, and Brooklyn's on the other side. Me and Nina poured us another drink and walked back to the ledge so we could dance and be seen.

I was already tipsy, but I was still drinking like a fish, knowing I'd be paying for it in the morning. Nina stood nearby, dancing with one of Quan's boys, so I stood off to the side alone, moving my body to "Needed Me."

"I guess my DJ is feeling Rihanna tonight," I thought to myself. But hey, it was perfect timing because I was feeling exactly how she was feeling on the song.

I was feeling the fuck out this song and sung it like I meant every fucking word making sure Brook felt me too. His eyes watched me and I couldn't lie, he was lookin bomb as fuck. But, I wouldn't bother to face him.

"Let me guess, you and your boy beefing right now?"

I turned around and Quan was in my ear with his arm wrapped around my waist. I was a bit nervous and shocked that he had become so bold because Brook had the city shook and niggas knew not to play or cross him.

I turned to face Quan and smiled flirtatiously. I was every bit of single and the alcohol wasn't making it any better.

"How you figure?" I asked, smiling all up in Quan's face.

"Well, one reason, y'all in separate sections, second, because I haven't seen y'all say two words to each other," he said and I felt kinda embarrassed. The last thing I needed was people knowing it was trouble in paradise, so I kept it nonchalant.

"It's whatever, honestly."

"Well, what's up, can a nigga get some of that good pussy for his birthday?" he asked, sounding half drunk.

His question caused me to laugh hard, showing all 32 of my pearly whites. When I stole a glance at Brook, he was watching me like a hawk, but the bitch Marie was all up in his face again and now my focus was far from Quan.

"Bitch, what's up?" Nina walked up, snatching me by my arm, and pulling me towards her.

"Like for real, Cash. I'm not feeling this shit yall doing."

"Fuck him, Nina!" I said, sneaking a peek in his direction.

"Cash, for real this bitch all up in his face. Just say the word and I'm a drag the hoe," Nina said with her fist balled up and she meant exactly that.

"Nah, ma, it's smooth."

"Ugh bitch, there go my boo," Nina said while looking over at this fine ass nigga coming up the stairs.

"Bitch, who's that?"
"That's Carlos from The Flat Line Projects," she said with lust in her eyes and walking towards him.

The moment he saw her, he wrapped his arms around her neck and bent down to kiss her. Indeed, he was fine as fuck and from what it looked, he had my girl open.

I shifted my focus back to Nino and that's exactly who he was acting like tonight. I leaned back on the ledge with my elbows rested on the railing and I shot daggers at him and his little groupie that was still all in his face.

Nicki Minaj and Meek Mills came booming through the speakers and I knew for sure he would come for me but to my surprise, he let that bitch sit right up on his face. It seemed like my liquor was getting the best of me now because I suddenly got depressed. When I looked back to his section, my mouth hit the floor. He had stood up and started dancing back with the bitch. Now I was really pissed.

This was our song, I couldn't believe Brooklyn was disrespecting me in my club. His friends weren't making shit any better, standing around cheering him on. I could feel the tears building up in my eyes, but I refused to cry in front of these niggas.

I stormed off to my office and ran to my desk. It felt like I had lost the war. I buried my head into my arms and the tears fell ninety going north. This shit was killing me. The last guy I really cried over was Carter. I had vowed from that day to never love again and here I was in my office, crying my eyes out.

Brooklyn

When I saw Cash run off, I felt like shit. No lie, it was all fun and games until that last look she shot me before running towards her office. The bitch Marie must've peeped game because she was smiling and tried to grab me, but I pushed that hoe so hard, she flew back and fell flat on her ass. I wasn't about to give that hoe the audacity to laugh at my bitch. What we were doing was wrong, but I ain't gone lie, the way she was smiling all up in Quan's face had me heated.

What made matters worst was that was a nigga she fucked before so that only made me want to beat both their ass right on the spot. Marie was pretty as a muthafucka, but not my type. She was just like the rest of these hoes, a sack chasing groupie. She had

192

been trying to get at me for years, but I never fucked ol girl and that's on my mama.

When I opened Cash's office door, she had her head inside her folded arms. I stood there until I couldn't take it anymore. Man, that shit hurt a nigga soul to see my baby cry, so there was only one thing I could do at this point and that was make shit better.

I walked to her desk and she didn't even hear me enter. Her office was dimly lit and she sobbed like she had lost her best friend. I picked her up in one swift move, sat her on top of the desk, and lifted up her blouse. I started tasting her body, starting with her neck. Her sobs turned into moans, but her face was still stained with tears. I felt so bad, I started apologizing and praying she wouldn't storm out on me like she had been doing.

"I'm sorry, little mama," I whispered to her, holding her head with both hands while looking her deeply in the eyes. It was like I could see my soul in them.

I kissed her forehead and she didn't bother to respond, which was good. She put her head down and her pout face was driving me crazy. She was literally the prettiest girl I'd ever seen and right now, she wasn't making it any better the way she puckered her lips. I lifted her shirt completely over her head, throwing it on her two seater couch. I didn't even bother to take her skirt off, I just slid it up and my hands followed.

I began fingering her pussy. Her head tilted backward and her moans were making my dick harder and harder. I couldn't take it anymore, I stepped out my shoes followed by my jeans. Cash wasn't no ratchet bitch so coming out all my shit was a must. Once I got completely naked, I stroked my dick a few times, and then pushed up in my baby's pretty pussy with ease.

I was hitting it for a few minutes, and it seemed like every time I stroked her more and more, tears fell down her face.

"Cash, stop crying, ma," I told her but it only made her cry more.

"I'm sorry, Brooklyn, I can't help it," she finally spoke.

I stopped pumping and attended to her needs. "I love you, Cash Lopez."

"I love you too, Brooklyn Carter," she said. I finally got a smile out of her.

She grabbed my dick and wrapped her entire mouth around it, damn near causing me to stumble back. It seemed as if Cash didn't have any flaws, her pussy was A1, her head was fire, and Lil Mama body was perfect. For a minute, I forgot we were still in the club until there was a knock at the door. When we didn't answer, the door came flying open and in walked Nina.

"Oh shit, my bad, yall," Nina said while walking into the restroom. It was like she wasn't even fazed by Cash blowing my top back because she kept straight.

When she walked back in, she started smiling. "I'm so glad yall not playing them childish as games anymore. Well, I'm leaving with Carlos." She walked to the desk, jotted some stuff down on a notepad, and slid the piece of paper in front us.

"Here is Carlo's full name and his phone number just in case he kidnaps me," she laughed. She walked right back out the door.

The minute she closed the door behind her, we were right back where we started. I picked Cash up and laid her across the desk, lifting her legs over my shoulders. I positioned myself between her legs and went for the gusto. For some reason, the night felt magical and it was sure of a night to never forget.

    ***

The next morning, I woke up to my phone ringing. It was Kelly, so I quickly answered because I knew exactly what it was about.

"Nino, you up, homie?"

"Yeah, I'm up," I said, getting out the bed and walking out the room so I didn't wake Cash.

"Well, I ain't gon hold you. I just wanted to tell you it's a for sure tonight."

"Oh, fasho."

That was music to my ears. We were about to tear some shit up. It had been months and Ricky must of have thought he was in the clear because he was having his party tonight as if I wasn't going to find out.

I wanted Cash to stay home so bad. I knew she was gangsta as fuck, but since I had caught feelings for her, I wanted her to stay out of harm's way.

My phone rang again, knocking me out my thoughts. When I looked at the caller ID, I quickly answered.

"Hello?"

"Hey, Brooklyn."

"How are you doing, Ms. Lopez?" I said to Cash's mom, on the other end of the phone.

When Cash was healing from her gunshot wounds, Ms. Lopez had reached out to me and we had become pretty close. I did know how she got my number but with the type of power she possessed in these streets, I knew it wasn't hard.

"How's my baby girl doing?"

"She's doing good. She's still asleep, you wanna talk to her?"

"Nah, its ok, don't wake her. So, you still babysitting your sister's kids tonight?" she asked, speaking on the hit on Ricky tonight, but speaking in codes.

"Yep, she just called me and confirmed."

"Ok, good. Brook?"

"Yes, Ms. Lopez?"

Trap Gyrl   Barbie Scott

"Make sure my baby straight out there, ok?"

"I got her, Ms. Lopez, you got my word."

"Ok, son. I'll talk to you in a couple days."

"Ok you take care ma," I said hanging up.

When I walked back in the room, Cash was awake, looking dead at me. I walked to my side of the bed and laid down beside her.

"Good morning, beautiful," I said. I brushed a piece of hair out her face.

"Good morning, Brooklyn," she bashfully said. That shit was so cute.

"Look, ma," I turned over to face her. "We can't be doing this shit to each other. Everything we presented to the world, we gotta keep doing. Cash, we're power couple and that's how this shit needs to remain. I'm sorry about everything. I know I fucked up, just tell me you forgive me? After I saw you cry, I knew I fucked up, ma. I promise, I'll never hurt you again," I gazed into her eyes.

"I'm sorry too, Brook. About everything! I hate beefing with you, I can't live without you. Just please promise me you won't disrespect me and give my loving away again?"

"I promise, ma. I love you and these bitches ain't worth losing you."

197

She kissed me. I laid back and pulled her on top of me. Damn, it felt good to have my baby back in my arms. Just the thought made me wrap my arms around her tight.

"Cash, you know we on tonight, right?"

"Good, cause its time for this nigga to meet his maker."

"I was hoping you'll sit this one out."

"Nigga, you know I'm not sitting down on this, Brook."

"I already know, ma. I just had to try my hand," I laughed.

"What time we rolling out?" she asked, sounding like a four-year-old going to Toys R Us.

"Kelly is going to call me when the nigga there. Then, we in and out."

I started running down the plan to her and after we were done, we went downstairs to take a swim and eat breakfast. We had an important night, so killing this nigga was a number one priority. We chilled in the house until it was time to roll out.

Chapter 16 *(Brooklyn)*

We got that call we been waiting on, so I got up after a nap and jumped in the shower. Cash was already up and I couldn't help but laugh because my baby was ready. She had on some black tights, her black Jordan 12's, and a black leather coat. I loved how she could switch it up and be a sexy girl or thuggish. She was a true soldier, it was like a gift and curse at the same time. It felt good to have somebody that could not only hold me down but hold her own without me. Then, there was that thought of something happening to her because she bled just like anybody else and this game wasn't built for a woman.

I'd heard about Cash years ago and always wanted to meet her, but she was the type of chick to intimidate any nigga that walked this earth. The night I ran into her at Esco's house, I already knew who she was but it wasn't the right time. I knew all about Ms. Cash, her club, her shop, and even her empire she ran as a boss.

When I met Mo, I didn't even know she worked for Cash but the bitch was so loose at the lips, that's all she talked about and that was my perfect chance.

When I got out the shower, I slid into my black Levis. I
started watching her as she sat on the bed, putting bullets in two
different guns. I walked to the closet and grabbed my 9 mm,
putting it on my hip, holding it with my belt straps. I tucked my
Glock in my band that was around my ankle. I then held my Tech
in my hand. I walked out with it so I could sit it on the floor in the
car.

When we got in the car, Cash turned on her girly gangsta
music, I guess that's what she called it.

As I drove, I let the words meditate my mind and even
rapped to Jay-Z part.

Jay did it with this one because right now I was living this
dream. I was a Boss ass nigga with the bossiest bitch in the game,
and I had plenty fucking money. Every time Beyoncé sang, Cash
would look over at me singing along and I could tell she was
feeling it. It was crazy because here we were, on our way to lay
some niggas down, and she looked as if he didn't have a worry in
the world.

"Cash."

"Yeah, bae?"

"Stay with me at all times, alright?"

"Got you," she said like she didn't want to hear the lecture she
thought was coming.

"I hope you listing, ma."

"I am, Brook. Damn, I got this."

"Yeah, alright, shawty." I just paid attention to the road and drove in silence until we reached our destination.

When we pulled up to the club, we parked in the back by the exit. This nigga was already inside so I dead the engine and made sure my straps were off safety. The initial plan was to run up in that bitch, but Cash thought it was best if we catching him coming out. It was now 1:42 and the club closed at 2:00 so any minute, this nigga would be walking out.

Blaze was on his way with Kelly, one of my Lieutenants. Just us four were all we needed because Ricky wasn't a major threat. He had a little squad, due to his dad's empire, but them niggas wasn't no killers. Hell, they weren't no trappers, they were flockers and that exactly what is was.

At 2:27 am, Ricky finally stumbled out the club. He had like six niggas with him. They all appeared to be drunk because they were staggering out of the club.

"Bae, are you ready?" I looked at Cash and she already had her strap in her hand.

"Let's do it, daddy."

We jumped out the car and creep through the alleyway. It was pitch dark, the only light was a glistening from the half of moon above us. Cash was right behind me as the party goers were heading straight to their vehicles. They were about to get the surprise of their lives.

I ran up on the two-door Tahoe. I saw him and his crew approaching. The moment I thought I had a good shot, I let my gun ring out...

"Pop! Pop! Pop! Pop! Pop! Pop! Pop! Pop! Pop! Pop! Pop! Pop! Pop! Pop! Pop! Pop! Pop! Pop! Pop! Pop! Pop! Pop! Pop! Pop! Pop! Pop! Pop!"

All you could hear were screams.

Two guys from Ricky's crew immediately whipped out and started blazing back, causing me to run and duck behind a car.

"Boom! Boom!"

I ran out towards the car again and got off some more, causing everybody in his entourage to hit the pavement. The niggas were bussing back, to my surprise, but that didn't stop me from shooting.

Surprisingly, I was sure they saw who it was, so they knew that the aftermath of this would turn sour. I was a real King and those niggas knew what I was capable of. But tonight, these hoe ass niggas was bringing back the beef.

When I looked back, Cash wasn't behind me. I started to panic, but I kept shooting.

"This shit playing out like a Steven Segal movie!" I thought to myself as I ran to duck for cover. *"And, this nigga must have beefed up his security.*

I began scanning my surroundings for Cash. Cash was a gangsta bitch so I knew she was straight, but I was still worried. After a few minutes of war with these niggas, I saw Cash running with a male figure who appeared to be Que. She jumped in a car that pulled up. I ran back towards my car while dropping two niggas in the process.

Ricky's bitch ass was protected tonight. However, I was confident I shot his ass in the midst of the war. As I was trying to make it back to my car safely, I looking back to make sure Cash was out of dodge. I was ready to chase these niggas and air out my third gun.

Cash

It was so much shooting. I had to run off from Brook to duck for cover. I was trying to get a good shot at Ricky while he moved cautiously through the crowd. It was hard for me to get a clear shot, so I began moving swiftly from car to car with my gun still pointed in his direction. Right when I had my barrel pointed at my prey, I knew I had the clearest shot to leave him leaking. At that point, I didn't care about torturing his ass, I just wanted him dead.

"Bitch, drop that gun," I heard a male voice behind me.

I turned around slowly and it was a security guard from the club. This old top flight ass nigga was about to play captain save-a-hoe. I was more than sure that he was a rookie because every security, at every club in the state, knew who the fuck I was.

He held his gun firmly, pointing it at my head. I bent down to lower my gun and grabbed the one in my ankle band. We stood face to face. The look he wore told me it was more than just club security. His finger went back slowly on the trigger and it seemed as if everything started moving in slow motion.

Pop! He actually pulled the trigger.

In an instant, I closed my eyes as tight as I could. I knew my life was over. It was like everything went black, I had lost the war and failed my team.

I opened my eyes when I realized I wasn't shot. I looked to the ground and security was laying on the floor bleeding from a bullet womb to his neck. Que was standing behind him with his gun smoking, this nigga never even seen him coming. I sighed in relief. I didn't have the time to talk because Blaze sped up in an unmarked car and we hopped in, doing about 80 MPH to get away from the scene. It was bodies everywhere, all you could hear is screams and cries from the patrons that were scrambling around trying to get to their vehicles.

"Where's Brooklyn?"

Que didn't say anything, so I looked at Blaze

"Blaze, where's Brooklyn?" I shouted in a panic. "We have to go back, Blaze. Turn around, we have to go back!"

"Calm down, ma, he straight. I saw him pulling off the minute you jumped in with us," Blaze said, looking back from the steering wheel.

I sighed in relief, looking over at Que who was silent and gazing out the window.

"How did yal know we were here?"

"Shit, we didn't. We heard this nigga was having a party tonight so we were gonna try and snatch his ass to take him to the chambers like you ordered," Blaze said, looking from me to the road ahead.

"That bitch ass nigga got away from us," I said. I was mad as a muthafucka. I slammed my fist into my hands.

"Yeah, his boys were strapped and ready."

"We on him now. I just hope he doesn't try and hide out like he been doing."

"Well, he knows for sure we on to his ass, so he just might."

"Thank you, Que," I said just above a whisper. I looked him in his eyes, trying to read him, and finally, his face softened and he spoke.

"No problem, Wifey," he said, causing me to smile.

I had to admit, I missed him and even my pet name he always called me.

As he continued to gaze out the window, I couldn't help but admire his gangsta. Even while in gangsta mode he looked so sexy. He must have sensed me looking at him because he smirked to himself, exposing his dimple.

"He think he slick," I thought to myself, smiling.

Blaze phone rang, interrupting my thoughts. He answered on the first ring. All I could hear was his end of the call. All he said was "yeah," then passed me the phone. I quickly took it, hoping it was Brooklyn.

"Hello?"

"Bae, you ok, right?"

"Yes, I'm fine."

"Where you at? I'm on my way to get you."

"We're pulling up to Que's house," I said in a nervous tone, looking over at Que, but he didn't even budge.

"Alright, I'm on my way."

"Ok…"

"Ma?" I heard Brook saying through the phone right when I was about to end the call.

"Yes?"

"I love you."

"I love you too," I said back, then disconnecting the call.

When we walked into Que's crib, me and Blaze went to sit at the kitchen table so we could hear Brook when he knocked. Que went upstairs then came back down in a little less than 5 mins carrying a duffle bag. He threw it across the table to me. I picked it up, knowing it was most likely the drops he collected this week.

"Who you collect from?"

"I haven't collected the trap houses money yet, that's from Mike, he came through and brought some work."

"Mike?" I said, unsure of why he was copping his own work. He worked for me for years and never did anything on his own. "What he cop for? Is he tryna do his own thing?"

"Shit, he just asked could he cop and he mentioned he talked to you already."

"Oh ok," I said, brushing it back but making a mental note to self to call him and see what was up.

Mike had been very distant lately. I knew it could have been because the problems he was having at home. He hadn't been showing up to his shifts lately, but I had so many workers that it was easy to fill in his spot.

"What if he found out about Blaze and Tiny?" I thought to myself, but hell no, all hell would have broken loose.

Que's intercom buzzed so I knew it was Brook at the security gate. Que told security to let him in so I remained seated at the table. When I heard him knock at the door I stood up, but Que beat me to it. He opened the door and stared at Brook with a facial expression I could read. However, he didn't faze Brook because he stared right back. When Que nodded his head towards the kitchen, I sighed lightly and walked back in to take a seat across from Blaze.

Brook walked up on Blaze and gave him a pound, then walked up to me and kissed my forehead. I felt kind of weird. I was praying nothing would transpire between the two and to my surprise, we talked about tonight's event without any problems. After talking over our plan, we got up to leave.

***

Almost a week had gone by and the streets were pretty quiet. I'd called Mike several times but the nigga wasn't answering. I called Tiny and she said he hasn't been coming home. Therefore, I was guessing, maybe he did find out about her and Blaze. However, I didn't want to jump to conclusions. Something was up with this nigga and I needed to find out. But, right now, I had to get ready for Niy Niy's Champagne party so I could surprise her with her car.

I scrambled around me and Brooks room for something to wear and needed to hurry before she made her grand entrance. When I talked to Nikki, she was doing her hair, and then she still had to get her makeup done. Therefore, I would be arriving just in time. Brook was out buying his niece a gift for her party that was tomorrow so he would be meeting me there.

It was the middle of May and the sun was shining bright, so decided on a pair of cut off stone washed shorts and a white mesh Gucci top with my white green and red Gucci sandals. I threw on a red blazer to give myself a sexy but sophisticated look and my messy bun exhilarated my outfit perfectly. I grabbed my gold frame Gucci glasses with the clear lenses and kept my jewelry simple. I wore my diamond studs and my little nameplate chain that read Brooklyn's name.

When I stepped outside, Niy's Benz was parked right by the door with a big red bow on top. I hit the alarm, ready to hop in when Pedro called my name.

"Cash, como estas, mi amor?"

"Como estas, Pedro?" I said smiling.

He motioned for me to come over. I sat my bag down in the passenger seat and proceeded his way.

"Cash, you have been on the go lately."

"I know, Pedro, it's been so much going on."

He looked at me with concern. "Mi Amor, do you ever think about getting out the game?"

That question caught me by surprise. "Honestly, I do sometimes, Pedro, but it's like the game needs me."

"I understand, I would just hate for something to happen to you. I know you're not a child anymore and Brooklyn will look after you, but this shit is watered down now."

"I understand and soon very soon, I'll be leaving this shit behind me, but right now, I have to keep my mother's business running because no one will run it with respect."

"Yes, now that part I do understand."

I looked at Pedro and he was aging so much. He had gotten old after his family was murdered and I knew because of the tragic death, he didn't want to lose the only thing he had left and that was me.

Pedro started off as my hit man, but I loved him like a father and I didn't want to see anything happen to him. I let him live in my pool house, which had three rooms and two bathrooms I had custom built. I tried to keep Pedro out of harm's way and prayed he would just sit back and live his life.

An older woman came out of the beach house and called Pedro over. My mouth dropped because this wasn't the maid and it damn sure wasn't no pool lady.

"Ooh, Pedro, you been hiding her, huh?" I said, laughing.

He smiled.

He motioned with his hand to tell her to give him a minute. The lady was a Hispanic descent with long black straight hair. You could tell that in her younger days she was a true dime and even now, as an older woman, she was beautiful.

My All Eyes On Me Ringtone went off, letting me know I had a text from Brook.

Bae: Hey, sexy, you dressed and ready?

Me: Yes, I'm getting in the car now.

Bae: Ok, I'll see you there, I'm leaving the mall, and then I gotta make one stop.

Me: Ok, bae, I'll see you there.

Bae: Ok.

"Ok, mi Amor, I'm going to let you go. We will talk later."

"I bet you will," I said, laughing and he smiled.

I was happy for Pedro. I don't know what is was with this chick, but I prayed she was more than a lady friend. It was time he moved on. It had been years since the death of his wife, and I wanted to see him happy again.

***

When I pulled up to Nikki's house, I was applauded. She had outdone herself with the decorations. Her husband had plenty money but the turnout was beautiful.

I stepped out the car and watched as the caterers moved around the yard setting up. There was a big banner of Niy from her younger year till now that read Niyliah's Prom 2016. It was a yard full of people and even Mo's hoe ass was here, but I didn't even bother to speak.

I walked up the driveway and made my way into the house, heading straight to Nikki's mini salon she had in the back of the house. I had always wondered why she didn't just work from home because her salon was decorated nicely and she had plenty clientele. Every time I asked her, she would say she enjoyed being at Trap Gyrl and she didn't want to be cooped up in the house all day doing hair.

"Hey, Boo," I said, giving Nikki a hug.

"Hi, aunty Cash!" Niy smiled, but she couldn't move because she was in the middle of makeup.

"Hi, Ti-Ti Baby," I said giving her a hug. I took a seat across from the two and watched how Nikki moved swiftly on Niy's makeup.

"Hey, Marvin," I said to Nikki's husband who was standing in the doorway, asking Nikki something about a cake.

"Hey, Cash!" he said, walking over to give me a hug. "You know I saw that, right? he smirked. I knew exactly what he was talking about.

I just winked and gave him a thumbs up.

"I'm going to go outside and mingle until you guys are done."

"Ok, I'll be done in about thirty mins, she just has to get dressed and were on our way out."

"Ok."

When I stepped outside, I said my hi's to a few people, and made my way to where Nina was sitting and to my surprise, she had Carlos with her. I sat at the table and made small talk with them while waiting for my baby to pull up. The entire time I talked to both, Nina and Carlos so he wouldn't feel left out.

Carlos seemed really cool and as if he was into Nina. I was happy for my girl because she had a glow about her. After the night at the club, I had Marcus run a full background on him and it actually came back clean. He was a gunner from the projects, two kids, and no girlfriend. His baby mama had a new husband, so that made me feel a lot better knowing my girl wouldn't have to deal with any baby mama drama.

When I looked over, Que was walking in with his bitch and he was carrying the car seat with their baby in it. I watched him as he approached a table, sitting the car seat on top, and Keisha took a seat right in front. When he looked my way, I quickly turned my head. I don't know why, but I was a bit jealous. However, I was pretty much over the entire situation. Nina was looking at me smiling. Therefore, I through my hands in the air in surrender.

I heard music out front, so I looked that way to be nosey and all I could do was smile. Brook's Maybach pulled up and the driver stepped out, opening the door for Brook. He stepped out looking like the Boss he was and I couldn't help but laugh because we were both dressed in red, white, and green Gucci everything.

His eyes scanned the yard until he found me. He closed the door and headed in the yard. All eyes were on him, he had bitches looking hard and whispering to each other. I stood up to greet him but he stopped at Que's table and they dapped each other. I was blown back, but smiling from ear to ear because they put all their bullshit aside. He was over to me and kissed me like we hadn't seen each other in days.

"Diva's!"

I knew that voice could only belong to one person, Diane. I jumped back up and ran over to her, giving her a hug, squeezing her tight. I missed my girl. Working as a Lawyer, she always busy and in and out of town.

"Awe, I miss you, ma," I said in a squeal.

"I miss you too," she was hugging me back, tightly.

"Damn, can I get in here," Nina said, walking up to hug Diane too.

"Where the rest of the girls?" she asked, referring to Niya and Tiny and truthfully, I didn't know how to respond.

Now, Tiny was at home stressed the fuck out and Niya was still doing Niya, fucking on any and everything she could get her hands on. She was back in school and that was a plus for her. She was in school to become a registered nurse, so between her school and clinical, she barely had time to do anything.

"Tiny is at home going through it with Mike's ass and Niya back in school, so I haven't seen much of the two lately."

"Well, I'm here for two weeks, bitches, turn me up!" Diane said. She as pumped up, causing everyone to laugh.

"Let's have a girl's night tomorrow?' Nina said, looking from me to Diane.

"Well, me and Brook are attending his sister's daughter birthday party but after, we can meet at my house and go for a late swim. I can get Julio cook up something."

"Bitch, you always trying to swim and shit!" Nina said, laughing.

I couldn't help but laugh harder because she wasn't lying. I loved water, rather it was a lake, beach, Jacuzzi or whatever. I really loved swimming because I felt rejuvenated afterward.

"Sounds like a plan," Diane smiled.

"What yall over here plotting on?" Brook walked up smiling and grabbing me around my waist.

"We're having a girl's night at my house tomorrow."

"Oh, is that right? Did you ask?" he said, and again, everyone laughed.

"Bae, you a hater," I said, playfully punching him in his side.

"So, can me and my boys join you guys?"

Nigga, it's not a girl's night if guys are there."

We all laughed again.

"Awe, that's fucked up. Well, me and the guys are going to go to Club Panties and see some ass shake," he smirked and looked at me.

"Yeah, and you can be leaving there in a body bag too," I said.

We all fell out laughing right when Que walked up and joined the conversation.

"Aye, Que, we're having guy's night tomorrow, you down?" Brook asked Que like they were the best of friends.

"I'm down," Que said, laughing. "Matter of fact, we are going to have it at my house, in my man cave."

Everybody laughed, looking at me because it was a No Cash rule.

"I'm coming with my bat too," I smirked and again we all laughed.

Two men emerged from the back, carrying red carpet and rolled it out. Nikki and Marvin came out first and stood to the side.

Everybody figured it was time, so we moved to where Nikki and Marvin were standing and patiently waited for Niy to exit the house. It was so many people and so many cameramen that it looked like paparazzi. I ran to the front and had my iPhone ready to snap a million pictures.

When Niy walked out, everybody was in awe. Her dress was flawless, something like out of a Mat Gala. It was silver with diamonds outlining the breast area, going down and around to her back. Her hair was pinned up with loose curls that fell around her pretty face.

When she stepped off the porch to begin walking down her red carpet, I walked right up on her to snap a selfie of us and stepped back to the side to post it on my Instagram.

When I looked behind the crowd, Brook was standing far back and I noticed some chick standing next to him. She said something to him that I couldn't hear. However, he brushed her off and he moved closer to the crowd, trying to get to where I stood. It was hard to get through because everybody was trying to take pictures, so I moved back to get closer to him. He grabbed my hand and in the process, I snapped a selfie of us together with him standing behind me, giving up a fuck you finger to the camera.

After everybody took their pics and she made it completely across the red carpet. Me and Brook followed behind her hand and hand and escorted her out to the front.

"Surprise, Niy-Niy!" I said, pointing to the car.

She stopped walking and her mouth dropped. "Aww, Aunty Cash, is this for me?"

"Yes baby, it's for you, I'm so proud of you."

"Thannnk you," she hugged me. She looked like she was going to cry.

"You're welcome, niece."

She walked up to the car and opened the door to exam the inside. I was so happy because she hadn't stopped smiling. I tossed her the keys and the tears came down her face, causing me to start crying. When I looked over, Nikki was crying too and Marvin was smiling.

"Thank you so much. Cash!" Nikki said, running over to me.

"You're welcome, ma."

We hugged each other while crying.

"What, yall tryna do make a thug cry and shit?" Brook said, and we laughed.

I wiped my tears away and Niy came back to me and hugged me again.

After Niy's Bentley pulled up to take her off to prom, we ate and sat around talking while enjoying the rest of the party. Slowly but surely, everybody started to leave. Shortly after, the sun went down, me and Brook left to head home.

I was good and drunk, and my pussy was throbbing like crazy, so I hit him off with the ultimate. I pulled his thick, long dick out of his white jeans while we were on the freeway.

Taking it into my mouth, I caused him to swerve a few times. I sucked it with ease, making sure to keep it good and wet. I handled it with care until he busted in my mouth and making sure not to get a drop on his pants. I had him going because the minute we walked in the house, he bent me right over the couch, not even giving me a chance to sit down my purse.

We made love all night from the living room to the bathroom, even in the hot tub until we were both tired and breathing hard.

Chapter 17 (*Brooklyn*)

I left Cash at home, asleep in the bed. That dope dick I gave her all night, she looked like she wasn't getting up anytime soon. I went to my Trap so I could collect some dough from Kelly. After I left Kelly, I was going to head back home to get dressed.

When I pulled up, I saw Kelly's Yukon and Bird's Impala parked out front. I dead the engine and made my way in.

"Sup, Boss?" Bird greeted me, giving me a pound.

"What's the word, y'all ready for me?"

"Yep, we are. We just got one problem," Kelly said.

My jaw tightened because I didn't have room for bad news.

"What's that, Kell?"

"Well, me and Bird are done with our work right here. I went to get Black's money and when I got back and counted it, it was short three stacks."

"Word?"

"Yeah, and this not the first time some shit came up short. I didn't want to say shit to you, but it's getting ridiculous, man. I can't keep covering for this nigga, Nino."

"So, what's wrong? Is he tricking off on them bitches?"

220

"Naw, worst than that, man. I think the nigga sucking that glass dick," Kell said like he was more than sure.

"Nah man, don't tell me that," I said while shaking my head.

I knew something was up with this nigga because the last time I collect from his trap, he was moving fast and jittery, and shit. Man, I hated to see Black go out like that. But fuck that, he was playing with my money and that's the one thing I did not tolerate.

"So, where that nigga at now?"
"He on his way. I called him to tell him I had more work, and that shit worked."

I couldn't help but laugh because Kell's lied to get him over here and that shit worked.

When Black finally arrived, he was shocked as hell to me standing behind the door. I walked right up on his ass and slapped his ass so hard that spit flew out his mouth.

"Wham!

He grabbed his face and his eyes told it all.

"Nigga, you fucking with that shit?"

"Nah, Nino. So, what you talking bout, man?"

"Nigga, you know what the fuck I'm talking bout. Why the fuck my money keeps coming up short?"

"I don't know, man, it was all there when I counted it," he said, insinuating Kelly was stealing from me, but I knew better than that. Kelly would never take from the team, I paid that nigga too good. Kelly had been down with the team since it was me and my brother's empire. After my brother got killed, he was still loyal to the soil.

I snatched that nigga up and started going through his pockets. I snatched his coat off his ass and just the look he had disgusted me, this nigga was looking like he weighed 100 pounds wet. When I turned his coat upside down, there it was. A glass pipe hit the table, and that nigga started crying. I slapped his ass again, knocking him to the ground. I stood over him with the pipe in my hand, shoving it in his face.

"So, this what the fuck you wanna do? You want to be a base head, nigga?"

"Nah, Nino, that's not mines, man. I swear it ain't mine."

"Nigga, shut the fuck up," I said, pulling out my strap and pointing it in his face. "Nigga, you're lucky I don't blow your fucking face off. Get the fuck out my spot, nigga!"

He quickly got up and scrambled to grab his belongings and the nigga even grabbed the pipe, sticking it in his coat. Right then and there, I knew he was in it too deep. As bad as I wanted to kill this nigga, I just couldn't. Black wasn't no enemy. Yeah, he stole from me, but the nigga had a problem and that shit hurt my heart.

I gave Black a job when he was 19. His mom and dad was on crack and had the young boy starving on the streets. I had to save the little nigga from Big Joe, who owned the neighborhood market because he had been stealing. When I asked him why he was stealing, he told me because he was hungry and hadn't eaten in two days. I felt bad for him, so I took him to get food and shook my head the entire time he devoured it. I then took him to the mall and cashed out on him some clothes and dropped him off to Kelly. He had been a part of the squad ever since.

"Damn, man," I said, still shaking my head.

"Some fucked up shit, Nino, it's only two things we could do, and that is to help him," Kelly, said looking at me.

"Nigga gotta help himself first, Kell," I grabbed the bags off the table and walked out.

When I made it to the door, Kell yelled out to me. I stopped in the doorway to holla back at him.

"You going to Britney's b-day party?"

"Yeah, I'll be through there later."

"Alright, one."

"Aye, Kell, send somebody to cover for Black and I'll hit you when I get up with Esco so you could go cop."

"Aight," he replied, and I was right back out the door.

When I made it back home, Cash was laying in bed cuddled up with Gutta watching TV. I couldn't help but laugh because she loved this damn dog like a real life baby and even played with it like it was a newborn. I took off my shoes and shirt, leaving on my basketball shorts, and joined her.

We laid there in silence. I hoped she couldn't tell something was bothering me. To my surprise, she didn't ask, and I guess from the look on her face, she had a million things running through her mind as well. It was only ten in the morning so we had plenty of time to lay around. I stroked Cash's hair with one hand while my other hand rested behind my head.

"What's wrong, Brook?"

"Nothing, ma, why you say that?"

"Because, that's the only time you stroke my head like that."

Damn, she had me to a science because she wasn't lying. Every time I was in deep thought, I would stroke her hair and stare at the ceiling.

"I'm good, ma, trust me," I ensured her and she snuggled closer up to me and continued watching TV.

I closed my eyes to shake the vision of Black holding that pipe, but I couldn't shake the thought at all.

"I can't believe my man's was going out like that," I thought to myself. I then closed my eyes for a nap.

***

When I pulled up to Lydia's house, it was a lot of cars parked out front. From where I was parked, I could see the top of a huge jumper and Ferris wheel. She through Britt a carnival themed party so there were bumper cars and all kinds of attractions for kids to ride.

Before I exited the car, I sent Cash a text to see how far behind she was. She texted me right back telling me she was pulling up. I stayed out front to wait for her. When she pulled up behind me, she exited the car and walked through the gate, bypassing the house, and going straight to the back yard.

When we reached the back yard, it was a yard full of kids having the time of their life. My nephew BJ spotted me and when he began running my way, he caused Britt and Bri to turn around. They both jumped out the bumper cars and ran to me to embrace me.

"Happy birthday, Britt," I said, handing her my gift.

"Thank you, uncle Brook," she smiled and walked off to sit her gift on the table.

BJ ran back over to the cars, leaving Bri-Bri behind. I scooped her up in one swift move and hugged her tightly. She looked at Cash and smiled.

"Uncle Brook, is this yo girlfriend?" she smiled, exposing her two front missing teeth.

I couldn't help but laugh because this girl was a hand full. Out of all three kids, she was Bronx's twin. She walked like him and was a crazy little something just like he was as a child.

"Yes, baby girl, this my girl, Cash. Cash, this is princess Bri-Bri."

"Your real name is Cash?" she asked, causing us to laugh again

"Yes, cutie, my real name is Cash," Cash said, pinching her cheeks.

"You're pretty, Cash."

"Thank you, Bri-Bri, you're pretty too. How old are you?"

"Five," she responded, holding up 5 fingers.

"Oh my God, five? You're so big for five," Cash said.

Bri giggled. She couldn't take her eyes off Cash and I knew after today, she would be asking for Cash every time she saw me.

"Bri, keep Cash company while I go find your mommy, ok?"

"Ok, Uncle. Cash, you wanna ride the bumper cars with me?"

"Sure, I'd love too."

I kissed Cash on the cheek and left them to go find Lydia.

I walked into the house, through the back door, and found Lydia in the kitchen over the stove. I walked up to her and pecked her on the cheek. I took a seat at the dinner table.

"Brooklyn, I'm so glad you came. Where's Cash?"

"She's outside with Bri."

"Oh boy, poor girl. Bri probably talking that girls ear off."

"You know she is."

We laughed.

"That girl is Bronx's twin, Brook. When I tell you she's a split image of that man," Lydia said while looking off into space.

"Yeah, I say that every time I see her."

"I miss him so much." Lydia looked like she wanted to cry.

"I know, Lydia. I miss him too."

No lie, I missed my brother to death. That nigga was my backbone, my right hand, my everything. I hated to talk about him or even think about him because that shit would fuck up my entire day. I had to get my mind off of it so I got up to go join Cash outside.

I stood in the doorway and admired my baby. She was breathtaking and the way she was handling Bri, made me really want to put a baby in her. She looked up and noticed me watching her, she licked her tongue out at me and smiled bashfully. They were standing in line to wait for their turn on the bumper cars. Bri was propped up on the railing and she played in Cash's hair. Whatever Bri was saying kept causing Cash to laugh. Her mouth was moving a mile a minute and her head kept tilting back and

forth, so I knew she was telling some kind of story. I walked over
to where they were and joined in.

After spending time with the fam, riding roller coasters and
driving bumper cars, we joined Lydia in the kitchen to grub.
Because it was a carnival theme, she had everything from popcorn,
hotdogs, cotton candy, nachos, and more. I was starving so I
pigged out on everything on the menu.

"Excuse me, Ms. Lydia, where's your restroom?" Cash
asked, standing up from the table.

"It's down the hall, fifth door to your right, doll."

"Ok, thanks," she said, walking off to find the restroom.

About ten minutes later, Cash came flying down the hall,
bumping into Lydia. When I looked at her, it looked like she had
been crying and was trying to run off.

"Cash, are you ok?" Ms. Lydia asked her in concern.

"Umm, yes, I'm fine," Cash said, but not making much eye
contact.

"Ma, you straight?" I asked her, getting up from the table.

"Yes, Brook, I'm fine. I have to go, something just came
up," she said and didn't even bother kissing me goodbye. She had a
worried look on her face and I'm no dummy, I knew my woman.
She was crying and I was about to get to the bottom of it.

"Excuse me, Lydia, I'll be back." I kissed Lydia her on the
cheek.

When I walked out to the front, Cash was nowhere in sight, just that fast, her car had vanished.

Chapter 18 *(Cash)*

I flew down Lydia's hall to the restroom. From all the juice and soda I had been drinking, it finally hit my bladder. I was really enjoying myself at the birthday party, having the time of my life with Brook's family. After using it, I washed my hands and checked my makeup because Bri was giving me a work out with her little self. I had to laugh to myself because her cute butt was a handful. I prayed because Brook was her uncle, and I didn't want my kids to be anything like her.

I made my way back down the hall, admiring her beautiful home. I stopped to look at a picture hanging on her wall that was a family portrait. I grabbed my mouth and I could feel my tears building up. I tried to keep from screaming, "I knew she looked familiar," I thought to myself.

It was a picture of Carter with Lydia standing next to him and all three kids in the front. Right next to it was a picture of Carter and Lydia kissing, standing in front of a Ferris wheel at on South Beach. I was stunned, my body froze and an electric shock ran completely through me. Carter and Brooklyn were brothers!

I tried flying out the door, bumping right into Lydia, but I kept going with a short response. I couldn't even look her in the

230

face. Brook was trying to stop me but I couldn't let him see me cry. Therefore, I ran by as fast as I could and jumped in my car to leave. My vision was blurred from all the crying but I managed to drive safely. I didn't have anywhere else to go so I jumped on the highway and prayed Nina would be home.

When I reached her house, her car was in the driveway, which didn't mean anything because she had multiple whips. I got out to ring the doorbell and to my surprise, she answered.

"Oh my God, Nina," I sobbed, falling into her arms.

She held on to me for dear life and closed the door with her foot.

"What's wrong, ma?" she asked, but I couldn't get one word out.

"Cash, please stop crying, you are scaring me."

When I could finally stop crying, I ran everything down to her from when I went to the restroom until I ran out and sped away from the house.

"Bitch! Oh my God. I don't know what to say"

"Me either, I don't know how to feel."

"Well, look, ma, it's not like you knew."

"True, but how am I gonna explain this to Brook?" I started crying again.

"So, are you gonna tell him?"

"I'm going to have to tell him, Nina. My conscious will eat me alive."

"You're right," she said, right when my phone rang.

I looked down and it was Brook calling for the 12th time since I had run out. I sent him to voicemail and he called right back. I couldn't keep dodging him, but for now, I was going to ignore him until I got my thought process together.

There was a knock at the door. I jumped up to run to the back but thank God, it was Diane. When she walked in, she could tell I had been crying. She kneeled down in front of me holding my hands in hers.

"What the fuck he do to you? Did he hit you? Do we have to jump his ass?" Diane said, causing me to giggle.

Diane was Italian, but she was hood and from the East Coast. She had moved to Miami for a job opportunity that turned into opening her own firm.

"No, ma, nothing like that."

"Oh ok, I was about to say, because you know ain't no punk bitches round here," she said, causing us to laugh again.

I just shot her a look that said listen up, and I had her undivided attention.

"Bitch, Brooklyn and Carter are brothers!"

"Wait, what fucking Carter, Carter Carter?"

"Yes, Carter, bitch!"

"Oh my God! How the fuck you find that out?" she asked. So again, I had to tell my story, but starting from the first time I saw Lydia.

I went to Nina's bar and poured me another shot of Hennessy. It was much needed.

We sat around and talked. I was so glad to be with my girls because they made me feel so much better.

Somebody started banging at the door while we were talking. I braced myself, but I was hoping it was just Niya and not Brooklyn. Brooklyn walked in the door, heading straight for me like a mad man.

"Bring your ass here, Cash!" he shouted.

I just looked at him and didn't move.

"Now!"

All the girls looked at me with an *ooh, you in trouble* look, so I got up and walked to him. He led me outside to Nina's patio and started with his third degree.

"What the fuck, ma? So you just run out on me and don't tell me what's up?"

"I'm sorry," I said above a whisper, looking down at the ground.

"So, what's up? Are you gonna keep beating around the bush? I called your fucking phone and you kept sending me to voicemail. I went home and you weren't there so I knew to come here to find your ass."

I sighed because I was scared to tell him, but I had no choice...

"Brooklyn, Carter is your brother," I quickly said and the tears came pouring down my face.

He stood puzzled like he didn't understand what I was saying.

"What you mean Carter is my brother, what Carter?"

"The Carter I used to be with," I said, sobbing.

"What the fuck are you saying, Cash?" his face tightened. He looked mad and sad at the same time, but he stood quietly.

After about two minutes of him collecting his chain of thoughts, he shook his head and stormed straight out the door without saying a word.

On my way home, I was in deep thought. I didn't know what to expect from Brook, but I was going to give him some time to himself. I prayed this wouldn't put a strain on our relationship but he needed to understand I didn't know Carter was his brother.

"How could I be so foolish?" I thought to myself.

It was all coming to me in a perfect sense. Carter's name was Bronx Carter and Brooklyn's last name was Carter. The time frame Brook had mentioned his brother had gotten killed went so perfectly with Carter's death. They resembled each other so much

234

from their athletic bodies to the dreads they wore, even their facial structures were the same. Damn! I cursed myself, feeling foolish.

My phone ringing non-stop broke my chain of thoughts and as bad as I didn't want to answer it, in the fear of it being Brook, I grabbed it out my bag. I was relieved to see it was Esco, but I curious to why Esco would be calling because we had enough work for the next two weeks.

"Hey, Esco?"

"Cash, get here now!"

"I'm on my…"

He cut me off. "Now!" he shouted and hung up.

I looked at the phone in disbelief. I don't know who the fuck this nigga thought he was, but he wasn't my man nor my daddy.

I headed straight to Esco's house as bad as I didn't want to. I wanted to go home, bury myself in my room, and turn off my phone but I knew it had to be something important. I was a bit tipsy from all the shots I had taken but not enough to swerve.

I made it safely and it's like the security was already waiting on me because soon as my car approached the big gate, it opened quickly. When I entered the home, I made my way down the long hallway to Esco's business room and took a seat to wait for him to enter. About 15 minutes later, he came in with a stern look on his face and leaned on his desk in front of me.

"Cash, Cash, Cash," he said looking me in my eyes. "We have a major problem, my love. Seems like you have a rat in your organization and rats are not good for business."

I looked at him with a curious look on my face. I wished this nigga would cut to the chase, but I remained silent and let him finish. "You need to handle this shit, and fast."

"No disrespect, Esco, but my soldiers are tight. I don't do business with anybody, and all my Lieutenants are loyal."

"Don't be so sure of that. Nobody is loyal in this game because the minute a muthafucker is in a bind, they will roll over on your ass faster than a blink of an eye."

"So, will you stop beating around the fucking bush and just tell me, Esco!"

"Young lady, don't take that tone with me," he said, but I wasn't trying to hear that shit.

"So, who is it, Esco?"

He shot me a look that said *you really wanna know*? before he spoke.

"It's Mike, Cash."

"Wait, what?" I said like I hadn't heard him.

"Yes, my love, your boy Mike. He's a fucking rat, Cash!"

"And, where are you getting this from?"

"Cash, look who you are talking to, don't you know my power? I have DA's, Secret Agent's, National Guard's and even

Judge's working for me, I find out about everything. Thanks to me, you're still out here and not in jail. You think them muthafuckas don't know about those bodies you have under your belt. I hear, I pay, and you're scot free."

I just looked at him with a firm expression, I knew he was serious. Now, I knew him and my mother was really close, but he didn't owe me shit, so why was he looking out for me like this? That was the question.

"Are we done, Esco? I gotta go."

I pulled out my phone and called Que, but he didn't answer. I called again and still no answer.

"Do you ever think about leaving this game, Cash?" he asked with concern. It was weird because I just had this same discussion with Pedro and he was asking the same questions.

"I have no choice, Esco," I said in a low tone and before I knew it, tears poured down my face.

It was like everything was hitting me at one time. The only two men I ever loved were brothers, one of my lieutenants was a supposed-to-be rat, and yes, I was tired of the game. Honestly, I'd been tired, I just couldn't let my mother down. I was the only one she trusted and that's why I was head of her organization.

Esco grabbed a Kleenex off his desk and passed it to me. He stood in front of me. He bent down and grabbed my chin, lifting it so I could look at him.

"My love, wipe your tears, this isn't you! You're strong, you can't show signs of weakness in this game or a mutherfucker will run all over you. If you want to leave this game, I'll help you leave it."

"I can't leave it," I said, standing up on my feet.

Esco was right, I had come this far so showing signs of weakness was out.

"Thank you, Esco," I made my way towards the door.

"Cash!" he called out to me.

I stopped and turned around slowly. "I love you, but I have to protect my business. Handle Mike or I'll have to cut you off," he said.

I knew he meant every word he spoke. I didn't bother to respond, I just walked out and closed the door behind me.

I called Que, and he still wasn't answering, but I was five minutes from his crib. I wanted to call Brook but I thought against it and shot Blaze a quick text.

Me: Meet me at Que's house, now!

Blaze: You straight, ma?

Me: Yes, just come on, ASAP!

When I pulled up to Que's house, I started to panic. It was swarming with police. It looked like the entire MPD was at his home. I hurried and called Blaze, but making sure I don't pull all the way up.

From where I was parked, I could see the entire scene. Que was being hauled off in cuffs and Keisha was holding her baby, yelling at the top of her lungs. At that moment, I felt bad for her.

They took Que to an unmarked car and before they shoved him in, he looked in my direction and paused. They shoved him around a little, pushing his head down into the car. He whispered the words *"I Love You,"* while looking in my direction, right when they were about to slam the door.

I sighed heavily and laid my head back on my head rest and for the 100th time that day, I cried.

Chapter 19 (*Que*)

I was sitting in a bitch ass integration room, ready to slap the fuck out this red neck ass cop that was yelling in my face so loud, spit was flying everywhere. I just sat there looking at his stupid ass like he was crazy. Nah, he was more than crazy, he was a muthafucking fool.

All he talked about was Cash, but what I didn't understand is if they had so much against her, why the fuck was I sitting here? Did they think I was going to tell on my right hand? Because if so, they had another thing coming. I was a hustler, I was a killer, hell, I was even a baby mama snatcher, but a bitch ass nigga is one thing I wasn't and any nigga that talk to the police was a bitch.

"So, Quintin, are you gonna stop bullshitting around and tell us what we need to know?"

"Fuck you!" I yelled at his cracker ass with so much force.

He ran up on me and snatched me up but his partner grabbed him, telling him to calm down. He walked away from me and started pacing the floor and his partner sat down and spoke like he had sense.

"Look, Que, man, I could make all go away if you just tell me about Cash Lopez. We know that's who you work for. You give us Cash, we will give you your freedom, all we need is a statement from you. If you give us a statement on this sheet of paper, your scot free," he slid the paper across the table to me.

I looked down at the paper, and then picked up the pencil that was beside it. I scribbled on it and signed my signature. After I was done, I slid the paper across to the officer, who name badge read Williams. He smiled devilish, but taking the paper from me. When he read it, his face turned red. He balled the paper up and rushed me so hard that he knocked me out the chair. I laughed so hard that his shove didn't even phase me. I had drawn a dick and pair of balls and wrote suck my dick underneath, that shit was funny.

"So, you think this a fucking game? You think this shit is a joke? We'll see if it's a joke when your ass locked away for the rest of your life and your bastard baby grow up without a father!"

This nigga was trying to make me mad but I didn't let him phase me. I looked at him and my lips curled up.

"You ain't got shit on me," I barked with confidence.

"Oh, I don't? You think I don't, huh? Remember those 32 keys Mike copped from you? Well, let's just say Mike works for us, you stupid black piece of shit!" he called me and didn't even give two fucks about his partner being black. What he hit me with

241

was some shit to leave a muthafucka shook up. I knew that shit wasn't true. *"Hell nah, not Mike,"* I thought to myself.

"Book him!" the cracker shouted, and the black officer immediately cuffed me.

After getting processed in, I was finally able to use the phone. I called Keisha to make sure she was straight because the way she was screaming while they were escorting me out had a nigga heart broken. Them muthafuckas were tearing my crib up so I knew my baby mama was still probably cleaning up.

"Hello?"

"You have a collect call from an inmate in the County Jail Facility, to accept the call dial 5 to…"

I immediately heard the phone pressing five.

"Hello?"

"Hey, bae," she said, sounding happy to talk to me, but I could tell she was stressed out.

"Sup, ma," I said quickly because I didn't have time for any mushy shit. "Call Cash for me on 3-way."

She smacked her lips and the way she was huffing and puffing into the phone let me know she had caught an attitude, but honestly, I didn't give a fuck. I needed to holler at Cash ASAP.

"What's the number?" she said in a sassy ass tone.

"Grab my phone off the fireplace and and get it."

"Hold on," she said and I could hear her moving around to do as told.

"I don't see Cash's number in here."

"It's under Wifey, Keish."

"Wifey, what the fuck?" she said with an attitude. "You foul as fuck, Que!"

"Just call the number, man."

She clicked over and for a second, I thought she had hung up until I could hear a phone ringing.

"Hello?" Cash answered on the second ring.

"Cash, what's up, ma?"

"Que!" she yelled into the phone. I could tell she was happy to talk to a nigga. I ain't gone lie, she had me smiling like a muthafucka.

"Yeah, baby girl, it's me," I said in my suave voice, and we both laughed. I almost forgot Keisha was on the phone until she huffed into the phone again. "Aye, ma, shit all bad, you hear me?"

"Yes..."

"This nigga Mike all bad."

"Yeah, I know. I'm going to handle it. But, how much is your bail?"

"Man, I don't even have one, but call Diane ASAP," I said while shaking my head.

"Alright, I'm going to call her now, don't trip."

"Alright, ma, love you."

"Love you too," she cooed and we both hung up.

You damn right I hung up on Keisha. I didn't feel like hearing that shit, I was already stressed enough.

Chapter 20 (*Brooklyn*)

Damn, I didn't know how to feel. I loved Cash like a muthafucka but the thought of her fucking with my brother didn't sit well with me. I didn't know if she knew and never told me. Either way, the situation wasn't cool.

As much as I tried to take my mind off it, I just couldn't shake the thought. My brother and I always talked about a chick he was fucking with but he failed to mention her name. All he would ever say was, *"Brook, I got a real Boss bitch, bro"* and we'd just laugh. I was always so busy, I never really had the time to meet her, now I wish I would have.

I picked up my phone to snoop on her Facebook like I did every time we were beefing. She had only written one status that said *Trust Nobody!* I didn't know what that shit meant so I brushed it off.

My phone buzzed on the dresser. I reached for it in a hurry, hoping it was Cash because we really needed to talk.

"Hello?"

"Aye, nigga?" Kelly said, in a serious tone.

"Sup, Kell?"

"Man, you holla at your girl?"

"Nah… why, what's up?"

"Nigga, her boy Que got knocked by the One's!"

"What?" I yelled, jumping up off the bed.

"Hell yeah, bout an hour ago. You need to make sure yo shorty straight."

"Alright, good looking, man."

"Don't trip, my nigga."

"Everything straight around there, right?"

"Yep. Quiet."

"Alright, I'll hit you up."

"Alright, one."

"One…"

I hung him up and dialed Cash, but she didn't answer. I didn't know if she was still upset, but shit was serious in these streets so I needed to make sure she was straight.

I hopped on the highway to head to her house. I wasn't sure what was going on, I just prayed she wouldn't be in cuffs by the time I arrived. I called her phone back to back and still no answer. I was sure that by now she had heard of Que getting knocked. However, what I didn't understand was why would she be acting immature at a time like this? The minute I got to her house, I was going to give her a piece of my mind because the entire thirty-minute drive had me stressed the fuck out.

When I pulled up, I was relieved to see the coast clear, but something was weird. The gate was wide open. Cash would never have her shit just open like an open house. I pulled out my strap and walked through her yard. It was so dark throughout her yard, I could barely see. I pulled out my phone to use it for light and made my way towards the house.

"Where the fuck is everybody?" I thought to myself as I approached the house slowly.

I didn't see any guards and that wasn't like Cash. Throughout the day, you would see security, gardeners, pool cleaners or somebody. Her shit was always busy, even when she wasn't home.

When I got to the side door, the house was pitch black as if the power was off. I walked through, still using my phone for light and checked every room. I heard a sudden noise coming from Cash's room. I held my gun in the air ready to shoot the first thing I saw.

I pushed the door open with my foot. I looked around the room and I was relieved to see it was Gutta. I scooped Gutta up in one swift move and made my way back down the stairs.

I walked to the pool house to look for any signs of Pedro. I scanned the rooms and I spotted Pedro laying on the floor covered in a pool of blood. I kneeled down beside him but his body had no movement. I checked his pulse and to my surprise, he had one. I pulled out my phone to call my private doctor and he had told me to bring Pedro ASAP. I was stressed the fuck out now because I didn't know where the fuck Cash was. Pedro was almost lifeless and I didn't know what the fuck was going on. At this point, all I could do was pray Pedro made it so I could get the full details. I said a silent prayer to myself, praying that Cash was ok.

Chapter 21 (*Cash*)

I was so stressed out after talking to Que. I went home to cry, and lay there in deep thought. I wanted to call Brook but I thought against it. Therefore, I did the only thing I could do when I was stressed, I went for a swim. I slipped into my Louis Vuitton two-piece, grabbed me a towel from the cabinet, poured myself a much-needed drink, and headed down to the pool.

When I made it down, to the pool, I took a big gulp and then eased down into the lukewarm water. After swimming a few laps, my body felt more relaxed. I swam to the edge to hit my drink and take a breath. That's when I heard a noise coming from the back of the house. I took a swig and sat the glass back down and out of nowhere, everything went black. I stood frozen, looking at my pitch black yard but I didn't see or hear any movement. I let my security go home for the night so it was just me and Pedro.

Pop!

I heard a single gunshot, so I stopped dead in my tracks. Fuck! I cursed myself because I had left my gun in my bedroom and my phone was in my purse, turned completely off.

I made my way towards the pool house where Pedro lived when all of sudden, I felt a pair of hands grab me. I was about to scream until I felt the cold steel pressed up against my temple. I didn't give a fuck because, in this game, it was kill or be killed. I knew I was playing with my life but at this moment, I didn't give a fuck. I started swarming, trying to get loose from the tight grip around my neck but I couldn't win.

After a few minutes of tussling with the intruder, I was hit over the head with what felt like his gun and everything went black.

2 hours later…

I could hear voices around me but I couldn't see shit because I was blindfolded. My feet were tied to my hands and I was gagged with what felt like a bandana.

"How long was I knocked out?" I thought to myself.

My head was pounding from all the bumping around during the drive which only made it worst. It seemed like we were driving for hours so I was in and out of sleep. I was freezing cold with nothing on but a two-piece bikini.

"These muthafuckas didn't even bother to grab my towel," I thought to myself, shivering.

The vehicle suddenly came to a stop. My body jerked hard, causing me to hit my head against the metal door because this muthafucka was driving like a bat out of hell. I could hear the doors open. I was yanked out and carried away.

I heard a sudden voice that put me in a frantic, and that voice belonged to none other than Ricky's bitch ass. I started screaming and kicking, but whoever was carrying me didn't bother to put me down. I was hit with a whiff of piss and what smelled like old sewer water that caused me to scrunch my nose. I was placed on a cold metal chair and in one swift move, my blindfold was snatched off. I stared into the cold eyes of Ricky and this muthafucka was wearing a smirk that read, *"Yeah, bitch, got you now."*

I coughed up as much spit as I could get and spat right in his face.

Whap! He slapped me, causing me to fall out the chair but that shit didn't faze me one bit.

"Oh, yo bitch ass finally showed up," I said, taunting him.

He smiled devilishly and smacked me again.

"Cash, Cash, Cash, you are a tough cookie."

"What the fuck you want, Ricky? Al, whatever the fuck yo name is."

"Oh, you know exactly who I am, hoe."

"You still ain't nobody, nigga! Fuck you, fuck yo daddy, and I swear I bet not get loose or I'ma kill yo bitch ass myself!"

"Damn, yall, this bitch got balls," the guy standing next to Ricky said while laughing.

"Yeah she do, man, but we gon' see how much balls she got after I stick my dick in every last hole on this bitch's body," Ricky said and the both of them laughed.

"Oh, so now you gonna rape me? I guess that's the only way you can get this good pussy, huh?"

"Whap!" He slapped me again. I guess I embarrassed him because his homie was laughing at his ass.

"Bitch, I don't even want yo pussy, I been through with that shit. You are about to get me rich, hoe. So, call your boy Nino and tell that bitch ass nigga I need five million or your ass gon' die," Ricky said, pulling out his phone.

"Fuck you!" I spat, but he just laughed again. These niggas thought shit was funny. I couldn't wait to get loose, I swear I was going to send Ricky to Hell with his father.

He put his gun to my head and dialed Nino's number. Five million was all he wanted, then he would get it. That type of money wasn't shit and damn sure not worth my life, but I knew better. Brook would bring him the money and he would for sure kill him and kill me, but I had to take my chances.

The phone rung three times and Brook answered. I could hear screams in his background that sounded like Pedro crying for help, I instantly panicked.

"Brook, are you ok?" I said in a panic.

"Bitch, I ain't got time for yall to be cupcaking, get to the point," Ricky said cocking his arm back. He then slapped me again.

"Cash?" I could hear Brook calling my name through the speaker phone.

"Guess who, bitch nigga?" Ricky said, snatching the phone out my hand.

"I swear, nigga, you lay a finger on her, watch!"

"Nigga, you still talking shit? I guess you don't love this bitch, huh?" Ricky said, laughing through the phone.

"If you were gonna kill her, she would have been dead, nigga, so how much you want?"

"Bitch, you guessed it," Ricky said, mimicking Lil Wayne's song. "I want five million, nigga, so drop that shit off at the Peter's Ditch. Come by yourself or your little boo gone be dead, nigga! Oh, and after I'm done with this pussy, you ain't gonna want this hoe again," he laughed like the devil himself. "Just to let you know I'm not playing…"

Pop!"

"Ahhh!" I screamed out in pain. When I looked down, my bikini top was covered in blood and it was flowing rapidly. *"This muthafucka shot me,"* I thought to myself, still howling in pain.

"You, bitch ass nigga!"

I could hear Brook yelling through the phone, but my body was drifting off.

"Pop! Pop! Pop!"

I could hear several gunshots again. I knew then my life was over. Slowly drifting, I was trying to remain strong but I was bleeding drastically and the pain was too much to bare.

I focused in on the body laying on the ground, but what was weird was it was Ricky's. With force, I scanned the room and noticed the other guy's body by the doorway. Then, out of nowhere, I was scooped up out the chair. My cries were becoming faint, but someone was carrying me outside. I prayed to God it was Brook but I knew it was too late.

I opened my eyes one last time, "Carter!" was all I could say before I drifted off into a dark place.

Epilogue

It had been three weeks since the incident with Cash. I felt like I wanted to kill myself because I failed to keep her safe. My whole world was crushed without her. I couldn't eat or sleep. Shit, I was cooped up in the house grieving to myself. Everybody came to check on me, but I pushed people away. At that point, I needed to be by myself so I could figure out my next move. I knew I had to shake this shit off sooner or later because my businesses couldn't run themselves but as bad as I tried, I couldn't get out the bed.

I had never loved a woman like I loved Cash, so moving on would be hard. All I did was scroll through her Instagram, looking at all her picture, then browsing her Facebook. As much as it broke me down, I still felt like she was near every time I read one of her statuses. The police hadn't found her body, but I was sure she was dead because I heard it with my own ears.

Ricky's bitch ass went back into hiding, but I had a five million-dollar price on his head. I knew in a matter of time, somebody would turn him in. I had greedy ass cops in my pocket, trying to get the money. Therefore, this shit was deeper than the Pacific Ocean.

Every day, Nina would call me, but she was making shit worse because all she did was cry. My heart went out to her friend's because they felt the same pain I felt.

I closed down her shops and gave Nina her keys, but I told her to wait a while before opening everything back up. We had to keep her business going in her memory, but right now was not the time.

"Ding!" I heard my doorbell but really didn't feel like moving. It could only be two people, Nina or Kelly because they came by every day to make sure I was straight.

I lifted out of bed and took my time, hoping they would just go away but I knew they wouldn't. I made my way to the front door and I could see a woman figure standing on the other side. She was an older lady but had a beautiful face and a nice body. However, what I wondered was who the fuck was she?

I flung the door open and she looked at me with a slight smile.

"May I help you?"

"Hi, are you Brooklyn?"

"Nah, Brooklyn don't live here. May I ask who are you?"

"Um, I'm looking for my daughter…"

"Your daughter?" I said like I didn't hear her. "Who's your daughter?"

"Cash, Cash Lopez," she said in a polite tone.

My body froze. Cash's mother was at the door and I didn't know how to tell her that her daughter was dead...

To be continued...

CPSIA information can be obtained
at www.ICGtesting.com
Printed in the USA
LVHW01s2319120618
580568LV00009B/281/P